Nisha marched up to him, her chin high.

She stopped so close he was sure she was about to poke him in the chest.

"I need you to know that you are not forgiven. You and me personally are not okay, and there is no way we will ever be. So tell me, Sameer, are you capable of behaving like a proper businessman?"

If anyone else had talked to him this way, he would've put them in their place. But as he looked at the fire in her eyes, all he felt was pride. The girl who'd unfailingly used "please" and "thank you," and who'd cowered when the local tea boy yelled at her for chipping a glass—that girl was standing up to him. He couldn't stop the smile that spread across his face.

He leaned forward and whispered so only she could hear. "I'm always a professional, Nisha. But with you? Never!"

* * *

Last Chance Reunion by Sophia Singh Sasson is part of the Nights at the Mahal series.

Dear Reader,

Thank you for taking the time to read my book. This is the third book in the series and Sameer has been there from the beginning. I'm excited to give him his chance at love.

A second chance at love is a story near to my heart. My husband and I dated when we were freshmen in college. As often happens with young love, we broke up because love was inconvenient at the time. We had our lives ahead of us and didn't really appreciate how special our relationship was. Fast forward more than a decade and we reconnected. We've been married for fourteen years.

It isn't as easy for Sameer and Nisha. Their past wounds are deep and ever present in their current lives. Forgiveness is not the hard part—believing in love is. I'm so excited to share their story with you.

Hearing from readers makes my day, so please email me at Sophia@SophiaSasson.com, tag me on Twitter @SophiaSasson, Instagram @Sophia_Singh_Sasson or Facebook/AuthorSophiaSasson, or find me on Goodreads or BookBub @SophiaSinghSasson. Head over to my website to grab a free ebook, SophiaSasson.com.

Love,

Sophia

SOPHIA SINGH SASSON

———

LAST CHANCE REUNION

HARLEQUIN

DESIRE

Recycling programs
for this product may
not exist in your area.

ISBN-13: 978-1-335-58143-3

Last Chance Reunion

Copyright © 2022 by Sophia Singh Sasson

All rights reserved. No part of this book may be used or reproduced in any
manner whatsoever without written permission except in the case of brief
quotations embodied in critical articles and reviews.

This is a work of fiction. Names, characters, places and incidents
are either the product of the author's imagination or are used fictitiously.
Any resemblance to actual persons, living or dead, businesses,
companies, events or locales is entirely coincidental.

For questions and comments about the quality of this book,
please contact us at CustomerService@Harlequin.com.

Harlequin Enterprises ULC
22 Adelaide St. West, 41st Floor
Toronto, Ontario M5H 4E3, Canada
www.Harlequin.com

Printed in U.S.A.

Sophia Singh Sasson puts her childhood habit of daydreaming to good use by writing stories she wishes will give you hope, make you laugh, cry and possibly snort tea from your nose. Born in Mumbai, she has lived in the Canary Islands and Toronto, and now currently resides in Washington, DC. She is the author of the Nights at the Mahal series and the State of the Union series. She loves to read, travel, bake cakes, make candles, scuba dive, watch foreign movies and hear from readers. Visit her at SophiaSasson.com.

Books by Sophia Singh Sasson

Harlequin Desire

Nights at the Mahal

Marriage by Arrangement
Running Away with the Bride
Last Chance Reunion

Texas Cattleman's Club

Boyfriend Lessons

Harlequin Heartwarming

State of the Union

The Senator's Daughter
Mending the Doctor's Heart

Visit her Author Profile page at Harlequin.com, or SophiaSasson.com, for more titles.

You can also find Sophia Singh Sasson on Facebook, along with other Harlequin Desire authors, at Facebook.com/harlequindesireauthors!

This book is dedicated to all those
who have needed a do-over,
and to my husband—for giving me
a second chance.

Acknowledgments

Thank you to the awesome Desire editorial team,
in particular Charles Griemsman, who has always
understood the nuances of desi culture.

It's lonely being an author but the amazing
community of South Asian romance writers
always keeps me going.

Last and most important,
I wouldn't be an author without the love
and support of YOU, my wonderful readers.
Thank you!

One

"Nisha, I'm not going to let you go without eating breakfast."

Nisha took a breath. She had to get out of her mother's house. Thirty more seconds and her mother, Reeta, would come barging through the bathroom door. She smoothed the foundation she had just dabbed on her face with a sponge and ran her fingers over her forehead. The big scar that used to cross from her right temple to above her left eyebrow was barely visible. Yet she could still feel the ugly red-and-brown mark that her mother had paid so much to remove.

She brushed some powder on her face, then a

touch of blush and eyeliner. Lip gloss would have to wait. She was already late.

As she opened the bathroom door, she came face-to-face with her mother, holding a bagel in one hand and her to-go cup of chai in the other. "Ma!" Her mother was half a foot shorter than her, which was saying a lot since she was only five foot seven, and thin as a reed with the same light brown complexion as Nisha. But that's where their similarity ended. Where Nisha had a generous wide mouth, her mother's was thin. Nisha had wide brown eyes while her mother's were rounder and a blacker brown.

"How are you going to have the energy to give your presentation without food in your stomach?"

Nisha sighed and took the cup and bagel. It was best not to argue.

"And is this what you're wearing?"

Nisha looked down at her standard black skirt suit with a Nehru-collared jacket. It was the same outfit she wore to every investor pitch meeting.

"What's wrong with this?"

"*Aaare*, you look too stiff. You should wear a dress, something sexy. And put on lipstick."

"Ma, I'm not going on a date, I'm trying to convince a very serious businessman to invest in my label."

"You never know when one of these meetings turns out to be a handsome, eligible *desi* bachelor."

Nisha had lost count of the number of times she'd told her mother that she had no interest in marriage, or dating. There was only one man she'd ever wanted to marry and she could still see the scars he'd given her. The only thing she was focused on right now was the successful launch of her label. For that she desperately needed this meeting to go well. Her business partner and best friend, Jessica, had told her that this was the last investor who had agreed to take a meeting with them. She had no more leads or contacts, and without a cash infusion, they wouldn't be able to put on a show for Fashion Week. Which pretty much meant a dead start. But trying to convince an Indian mother with a thirty-year-old daughter that she shouldn't worry about getting her married was like telling a small child on Christmas Day that Santa didn't exist.

"Ma, I'm getting late."

"But, Nisha."

"Love you, Ma." She gave her mother a peck on the cheek, then raced out of the two-bedroom Manhattan condo they shared. By New York standards, they lived in the lap of luxury with an eight-hundred-square-foot apartment in East Village. She was the envy of her staff and friends but only she knew what it had really cost her mother. The familiar pang of guilt sliced through her. While her mother irritated her on a daily basis, she had given up a lot to support Nisha. Too much. Which was all the more reason she had to launch her label successfully. She never wanted to be in a situation where she had to depend on a man for her future.

She looked at her smart watch as she rode the elevator down, clutching a large leather portfolio bag. It had been a gift from her mother when she'd first announced what she was going to do with her life. It was engraved with two simple words in the Devanagari script used for Hindi. *Khush raho.* Stay happy. Not be happy. Stay happy.

They lived on the nineteenth floor and she crossed her fingers that the elevator wouldn't stop on every floor. Like the rest of the building, the elevator was far from New York chic. More *Downton Abbey* stuffy. There were gold crown moldings, a threadbare Oriental rug and faded wallpaper. The required elevator certificate stuck out like charcoal stains on a white dress.

As she exited the building, she waved toward the doorman, who immediately understood her signal and waved down a pedicab. The iconic yellow cabs were getting fewer and fewer as Uber and Lyft took over the city but she loved the pedicabs. The bicyclists could weave through traffic the way no car could, and it was the fastest way to cover the two miles to her studio. She climbed onto the seat and gave the tall golden-haired bicyclist directions.

He dropped her off at Tenth Avenue and West Thirteenth Street, and she expertly avoided stepping in the pothole that had nearly claimed her ankle several months ago.

As soon as she entered, Jessica accosted her. "Just in time. We have exactly an hour before the investor arrives. The models will be here in half an hour."

Nisha gave Jessica a grateful smile, knowing her partner had been here for at least a couple of hours, crunching numbers and making dynamic data charts to wow the investor. Nisha was the creative part of their fashion line while Jessica did everything else. She knew Jessica had spent countless hours planning the investor pitch session and finding ways to save them every penny she could. Paying for the models, makeup artist and the styling staff cost a lot, and most of their meetings got them nothing. This was their last chance to raise the money they needed in time for Fashion Week.

"I looked at the outfits you picked. If I can make a suggestion, I think you should include more of your Indian-inspired designs, like maybe that yellow-and-royal-blue one. The colors are so unusual and striking."

"That's a little risky."

"Not for this investor. He's Indian and he said he liked your bold style when I sent him the prospectus."

"What company is he from?" Nisha didn't know why her pulse quickened every time she heard of a rich Indian family. There were tons of wealthy South Asian investors. She'd moved on with her life. Settled into a new country. Why couldn't she just delete Sameer Singh from her mind? Why did he keep popping up like a pimple on picture day?

Jessica nodded. "From the Mahal hotels investment group. Their only condition is that if they agree to invest, we hold our Fashion Week show at their newly acquired New York hotel."

Nisha relaxed just a smidge. The last she knew of Sameer's family, they didn't own any hotels in the United States. All their properties were in India.

"Is that condition worth it?"

"Beggars can't be choosers. It's not an ideal location but that's what makes this a desirable deal for them. I don't have any more leads. They're even willing to include the event expenses as part of their investment and if the first event goes well, they have a property in Vegas where they'll host another show. Honestly, that alone is huge. With the savings in show expenses, we can hire a few more seamstresses and embroiderers for those designs that I told you were too expensive to do."

Nisha bit her lip, trying not to let the bubble of panic forming in her stomach rise to her throat. They needed this investment. No matter what. The designs Jessica had nixed were unique and fabulous and if the coming investor could make that happen, then she would do whatever it took to convince him.

They spent the next hour getting ready for the mini fashion show they'd put on for the investor. When the time approached, they were ready and Nisha took a deep breath to cleanse her mind of the preceding chaos to get the models ready and styled. It was a technique that her mother had taught her from years of doing yoga. Not the new age crap that studios around the city peddled in a gross display of cultural appropriation but the real kind where she could focus her mind and direct positive energy into her body to prepare for the coming stress.

They stood at the doorway, waiting for their guest. "Who is representing the Mahal Group?"

"A Mr. Singh," Jessica answered.

Nisha froze as a chauffeur-driven town car pulled up before the front door. Singh was a very common name among Indians from Northeast India. It couldn't possibly be Sameer. *But how many billionaire hoteliers named Singh are there in the world?*

When she saw the man who exited the car, her stomach untwisted. It was not Sameer Singh. He was way too short, and a little too stocky. Sameer towered over her, his body lean and athletic. His chest muscular, and worthy of nighttime fantasies. It had been eight years since she'd seen him, but she would recognize him anywhere. At the main entrance to the door, she stepped forward with a smile on her face.

"Mr. Singh, I'm Nisha Chawla. Thank you so much for your time today."

The man smiled and shook her hand. He spoke with a thick Indian accent, much like her mother. "Most pleased to meet you, ma'am, but I'm not Mr. Singh. My name is Vinod Sharma. I'm Mr. Arjun Singh's personal assistant."

Nisha's heart dropped to her toes. Now that was

too much of a coincidence. Sameer had an older brother named Arjun. His family owned hotels in India. Had they expanded to the United States? She stood mutely trying to process what she'd just heard. Jessica handled all the business dealings and they had so many of these meetings, Nisha couldn't keep track of all of the investors. Now she wished she'd asked more questions earlier.

Jessica stepped forward. "I'm Jessica. We've been corresponding over email and phone."

He pumped her hand. "Mr. Singh will be coming soon."

If it was Arjun, Nisha could handle it. She'd met him several times; he was cold and shrewd but he wasn't Sameer. Still, her stomach wouldn't stop churning. *This is why Ma always insists I have breakfast.*

A motorcycle roared to a stop behind the town car. Nisha's heart stopped. The figure on the motorcycle had a full-face helmet and a black business suit but even before he turned off the engine and engaged the kickstand, she knew it was Sameer. She knew by the way he moved, the way his fingers combed through his hair when he took off his helmet and the way her chest tightened so much that she couldn't breathe.

"Ah, there's Mr. Singh, very good."

Nisha's feet were glued to the ground. Jessica elbowed her, then went to the door. "I'll give the

driver parking instructions. Nisha can start showing you around."

Nisha didn't register anything she said. She
stared disbelievingly as her first lover, the man who
still haunted her dreams, the one she remembered
every time she looked in the mirror and saw the
scar on her face, strode toward her with a brilliant
smile on his face.

His expression didn't register the surprise that
she was feeling. He stopped in front of her and put
his hands on her shoulders. "Nisha, it's so good to
see you after all this time."

He leaned in to give her a hug and she stepped
back, pushing his arms away roughly. "How dare
you show up here."

Two

Sameer smiled at Nisha. He knew she wouldn't be pleased to see him and he couldn't blame her. He stepped back and held his hands up. "Sorry, I thought we were old friends, I didn't mean to invade your personal space."

She glared at him. *Had she always had such fire in her eyes?* The answer came to him in the quick flash of a memory. The two of them in a hotel room in Mumbai, the moan from her throat, the softness of her skin underneath his bare chest, the feel of her legs around him; the blaze in her eyes as he made love to her. He took another step back from her, surprised by the intensity of the memory. It had been eight years. So much had happened, he hadn't once considered that his feelings for her might not have changed.

"We are not friends, and never will be. If I'd known this meeting was with you, I would've told Jessica not to bother. How dare you think you can waltz into *my* studio..."

She stopped as Jessica put a hand on her shoulder. "Nisha, can I talk to you privately?"

Nisha took a shuddering breath and Sameer felt the urge to grab her by the shoulders and tell her to calm down like he used to do in college when she got angry. Jessica led Nisha away and Sameer smiled as he watched them through the glass wall of the office. The studio was an industrial warehouse that had been made trendy. The high ceiling with its exposed pipes and ductwork had been painted black. Modern chandeliers with naked bulbs shone directly on the worktables littered with fabrics, sewing machines and pattern papers. In the center of the warehouse, a narrow red carpet formed a T shape. Foldable chairs had been placed at the horizontal end of the T. As far as investments went, Nisha's business wasn't a great one. The studio was stylish but they didn't have a Fashion Avenue presence with a glittery storefront. That lack of visibility was why Nisha's talent hadn't really gone anywhere.

The glass office was surprisingly soundproof. Either that or Jessica and Nisha were furiously whispering. He smiled at the familiar hand gestures and the way she pursed her lips. She hated when she wasn't in control of the situation. He hadn't wanted to take this meeting either but at least he'd known he would be facing her. She clearly had not been prepared to see him.

When he saw Nisha square her shoulders, he knew she wasn't kicking him out. She marched up to him, her chin high, and for the first time he noticed that she was much shorter than he was. He looked down to see that she was wearing flats. The only time he'd seen her without heels on was the night they'd shared a hotel room. Another image flooded his mind: her naked on the phone ordering room service chai as he wrapped his arms around her, his body hard against her cool, soft skin. His body heated at the thought of how her small figure curved into him. *Sudhar ja, Sameer!* He scolded himself to behave. Nisha was off-limits. Far off-limits. Not only had he already broken her heart and her body, but she was now his one chance to prove to his family that he was ready to be the responsible adult he should have been all along. They'd given him so many chances. It was time for him to show that he was worthy of their love and support.

Nisha stopped so close to him that he was sure she was about to poke him in the chest. "I need you to know that you're not forgiven. You and I personally are not okay, and there is no way we will ever be. But Jessica has worked really hard on today's presentation, and I understand you are a legitimate investor. So tell me, Sameer, are you capable of be-having like a proper businessman?"

If anyone else had talked to him this way, he would've put them in their place. But as he looked at the fire in her eyes, all he felt was pride. The girl who unfailingly used *please* and *thank you*, and cowered when the local tea boy yelled at her for chipping a glass, was standing up to him. He couldn't stop the smile that spread across his face. He leaned forward and whispered so only she could hear. "I'm always a professional, Nisha. But with you…never!"

Her eyes narrowed but before she could say anything, Jessica smoothly stepped up to them. "Mr. Singh, how about we start with the show. Our models are ready."

He turned to Nisha, who refused to meet his gaze. He recognized the slight press of her lips. She needed time to cool down. Jessica directed him and Vinod to sit in the folding chairs.

Nisha stalked to the other end of the room where room dividers had been set up. He could see her talking with two tall women, their heads visible above the dividers. Jessica began talking about how their business started and the inspiration for Ni-sha's designs. Then she cued the music and one of the models walked down the red carpet wearing a stunning royal blue dress with silver embroidery. She walked down the makeshift runway and posed. Sameer tried to focus on the designs but his eyes were glued to Nisha adjusting the clothes on the other model.

All of the clothes looked fabulous. He hadn't expected anything less. His mind wandered back to when they were in college.

"See this hemline, Sameer? If I'd designed this dress, I would have made it asymmetrical to complement the pattern here." He looked in the mirror as she twirled in front of it.

"Once I'm done with college, I'm going to model. I want to see my face on the world's top fashion magazine. Maybe I'll even break out on the international stage as the first average-height model."

"Your mother will never let you walk down a runway wearing clothes with low necklines and high hemlines."

"She can't stop me. Nobody can."

He watched as her hands worked furiously to button a blouse worn by the tall brunette. Nisha hadn't become a model. Because of him. He mentally shook his head. He wasn't going to fall into the self-loathing spiral again. This was his chance to make amends to Nisha. He'd make sure her fashion label was successful. He owed her that. It was his do-over, and he was going to make sure he used it well.

"Initial thoughts, Mr. Singh?"

Sameer forced himself to turn to Jessica and gave her his most charming smile. "Please call me Sameer."

She returned his smile and he noticed from the corner of his eye that Nisha was staring at them. "I think it's time we talk numbers."

Jessica gave him a wide smile. She was an attractive woman, with bright blue eyes and dirty blond hair styled back from her face to show off her cheekbones. If Nisha wasn't in the room, he'd have found her attractive. But even now, whenever Nisha was around, he found it hard to notice, let alone focus on another woman. Yet he forced himself to do exactly that now. Jessica was Nisha's partner and didn't know him. She didn't have history with him. She'd be the one to convince Nisha to give him a chance.

Jessica excused the models and directed him and Vinod to an office. As they entered, Sameer could tell this was Nisha's office. It was decorated simply but elegantly with a white desk at one end and a set of comfortable blue-and-white-striped sitting chairs arranged in a square around a reclaimed wood coffee table. There was a stack of papers on the desk. Photographs of dresses and artistically framed fabrics hung on the walls in perfect asymmetric harmony. It reminded him of her room in college.

Jessica handed out folders and directed them to the budget pages. "Now that you've seen the talent of our business, let me explain our plan to make you money. First…"

As Jessica talked, Sameer studied the files that she'd handed out, trying to resist the urge to look at

Nisha, who was standing at the door like a scared horse ready to bolt at the first provocation. His heart hadn't stopped hammering since he'd first walked through the door. He'd expected to feel something but he hadn't been prepared for the avalanche of emotions storming through his body.

Sameer forced himself to focus on the papers in front of him. He didn't want to face the contempt he knew he'd find in Nisha's eyes. He had one job to do, and that was to make her label a success. He needed to channel his brother's business ruthlessness.

He went back and forth with Jessica on the numbers, then they discussed the details of the first show, which would be the major launch for Nisha's label. He asked a question and Jessica turned to Nisha. "What do you think?"

Nisha seemed to be caught off guard. "Can you please summarize the issue for me again?"

"The original proposal was to do your Fashion Week show at the Mahal hotel here in New York. But now that we've looked at the specs, the hotel is too small. Sameer is suggesting that we still have it there but make it ultra-exclusive with limited invitations rather than finding another venue."

Nisha shook her head. "This is my first show. I need as much exposure as possible. That means a big venue so that everyone who wants to come, can. If the hotel isn't big enough, we can use our backup location. There's a warehouse in Brooklyn…"

"Nisha, if I may…" Sameer interrupted.

Nisha glared at him, her eyes shooting daggers into his heart.

"For your first show, a central Manhattan location is key. You want to be close to the other shows because people go from one to the other. No one is going to go out of their way to attend a new designer's presentation. And if you have more seats than people, that looks bad. Once the word gets out that this show is so exclusive that tickets are hard to get, the bigger names will want to be there."

Nisha shook her head. "That works for the known fashion labels. It doesn't for new names like me."

"But you're not a new name. Your designs have been featured in *Vogue*, and you've designed for Bollywood actresses. I think there will be a lot of interest in the show and making it small will create just the kind of frenzy you need to get serious attention."

"Excuse me, Sameer, but how much experience do you have in the fashion industry?"

"I know business, Nisha."

"But you don't know me."

Ouch. I don't? Don't I know that you agree with me but you're going to hold your ground because you want to show me how strong you are? It was just like the time in college when they were playing truth or dare. She'd taken a dare and their friends asked her to break into a neighbor's house and jump into the pool. Nisha couldn't swim so he'd offered to do the dare for her but she'd refused. By some miracle, the pool wasn't as deep as they thought but she came up sputtering, barely able to keep her head above the water. She managed to drink enough pool water to be sick the next day but not once did she regret taking the jump.

Jessica cut in. "Why don't we leave the discussion of the location and move on to other items. We can come back to this in the final negotiations once Nisha and I have had a chance to consider the space."

Nisha turned and walked out. Sameer watched through the glass walls as she went to the kitchenette at the other end of the room. For the first time, he noticed something was off with her gait and wondered whether she hadn't fully recovered from the accident. Was that why she'd stopped wearing heels? He knew she had fractured her leg pretty badly and had required surgery but his mother had said that she was fully healed now.

He watched as she opened the refrigerator and grabbed a bottle of water. She took a long swig and held the bottle in her hands, then suddenly looked up and met his gaze.

He stood, tugged down his jacket and strode toward her.

Nisha straightened as he approached, her face steely. She stepped behind the small round eating table. He stopped at the edge of the table, keeping it between them. It was for the best that he didn't get too close to her.

"This is your company, is it not?"

The question made her stand up straighter and cracked the icy composure of her face. She lifted her chin, which he took for an answer.

"And you need money to make sure it stays solvent, do you not?"

This time she blinked. "We don't need your money."

"The numbers your business partner just presented say otherwise," he said evenly.

"I said we don't need *your* money."

"It's not my money. It belongs to my family."

Her nostrils flared ever so slightly and she narrowed her beautiful brown eyes. He leaned over the table, pushing his face as close as he could get to hers. His eyes dared her to take a step back but she stood her ground.

"You need their money. There's no time to find another investor, and you have too much talent to waste it with your *zid*."

The narrowing of her eyes told him that she didn't appreciate being called stubborn.

"Why now, Sameer?" Her voice was laced with contempt. "You haven't bothered with me for eight years. Why now?"

"It wasn't my idea," he said quietly. He'd like to tell her that he'd thought of her nearly every day in the past eight years. That he'd been too self-centered and afraid to know how to face her. Then this opportunity had fallen in his lap. His sister Divya had come up with the idea to invest in South Asian artists as a way to expand their business and support *desis*. When Nisha's name came up, he'd thought hard about whether he could handle doing business with Nisha. But then he realized it was the universe's way of giving him another chance. An apology wasn't going to win him Nisha's forgiveness or his own. He had to give her back what he'd taken: her dreams.

"Look, Nisha, I know the last eight years haven't been easy on you, but I haven't had it easy either."

She narrowed her eyes. "Sure seems like you had a lot of time to party from your social media posts."

So she's been keeping tabs on me.

"It's more complicated than that. I just got out of rehab nine months ago and this is the first business venture I'm taking on. Divya and Arjun want to support *desi* artists and I can't think of anyone more deserving than you. This is not just your opportunity to launch your label, it's also mine. I need to prove that I've finally stopped being a fuckup."

He hadn't meant to say all that but his normally spectacular ability to bullshit seemed to crumble with her staring at him like she could read his mind. He looked away, unable to see the pity that would surely replace the anger in her eyes. He had three interfering sisters, a dictatorial older brother, a stubborn father, and an overprotective mother and sister-in-law. It had taken a long time for him to trust them enough to share his problem with them, and even longer to convince his family that he would work hard every day to make sure he never had to go to rehab again. He'd had enough attention and pity to last him a lifetime.

"So once again this is all about you?"

He turned to see the fire in her eyes, harsher than before. There wasn't an ounce of sympathy on her face.

She leaned forward so now their faces were just a few inches from each other. "You treat me like shit and then you come here with a sob story expecting me to feel sorry for you?"

He smiled. "I don't need your pity. I need you to stop being so stubborn, and see that this is a win-win situation. Not only do you get the money you need for your business, but you get an investor who owes you one."

She scoffed. "One? You owe me a few dozen."

He had her. As hard as she was trying to keep her face frozen, there was a crack in the seam. Sameer didn't do business like his brother, Arjun, but there was one very important lesson he'd learned from his tough older brother.

When to walk away and make *them* chase *you*.

Three

"Nisha, have you lost your mind?"

Nisha closed her eyes. It wasn't often that Jessica freaked out but that's exactly what she was doing, minutes after Sameer had walked off with barely a goodbye. He'd donned his motorcycle helmet and ridden off like he was the tragic hero of a B-rated Bollywood movie. Vinod had apologetically rushed out with a promise to call Jessica.

"How could you bring him in as an investor?"

Jessica put a hand on her hip. "Vinod and Arjun were the only contact names I had. You never told me Sameer's brother's name was Arjun. Singh is such a common last name, I didn't think twice about it. Still, there was no reason to behave the way you did."

"Jessica, you have no idea of the history between us."

"I know all about it. He's the love of your life from college who slept with you, broke up with you over drinks the next evening and then drove both of you into an accident that injured you and killed your dreams of being a model."

"When you say it like that, it sounds like he snapped gum in my face."

Jessica released a breath. "Look, I don't mean to trivialize what happened, but you've said yourself that the accident wasn't his fault. You were drunk and insisted he drive. And the other driver veered into your lane. Can't you find a way to work with him?"

"You don't understand. It's not about the accident. Losing my virginity was a big deal. It isn't like it is here where college coeds are anxious to get rid of their last reminder of adolescence. In India, girls are taught to hold on to their cherry until the right man comes along. I thought Sameer was it. We'd been friends since secondary school. He knew what sleeping together meant to me. If he wasn't there emotionally, he shouldn't have done it. He betrayed our friendship, reduced my love to a one-night stand. How do you expect me to forgive him for that?"

Jessica put a hand on her shoulder as Nisha buried her face in her own hands. Why did he have to come back? She'd been doing fine. In the last two years, she'd managed to date and even enjoy sex with men. Her every waking thought had not been about Sameer. But now he was back, and testing her resolve to forget he ever existed.

"Hey, men are pigs, that's for sure. But, Nisha, you've worked so hard for this label and you're so close. He's the only one left who can get us the money in time to get in on Fashion Week. And frankly, having his brother's hotels host additional shows is a big bonus. We can't ask for a better investor. We are so close. Are you going to let him have the power to stop you from achieving your dreams? Come on, you're stronger than that."

Nisha looked at Jessica. She couldn't take all the credit for where they were. Jessica had been a successful hedge fund manager on Wall Street when Nisha had talked her into quitting her job to partner with her. Jessica handled all of the business aspects of the label, working day and night to market Nisha's designs and get her important celebrity dressing opportunities. Nisha wouldn't be where she was without Jessica and she owed it to her friend not to tank everything because she couldn't control her heart.

"Can you make it so that I don't have to work with him?"

Jessica blew out a sigh of relief. "I'll deal with him, don't worry." Then she smiled. "Plus, you know what the best revenge is for a man who broke your heart? To let them see you successful and happy. Can you imagine Sameer's face when he sees your blond hottie?"

Nisha smiled. She had been dating this one guy on and off whom she wouldn't dare introduce to her mother. But she wouldn't mind showing Sameer that she'd moved on.

"I guess we better get to work." Nisha felt a new surge of energy. Jessica was right. She could handle Sameer. What she needed to focus on now was the fact she had the cash infusion she needed to get her new designs made in time for Fashion Week.

Nisha sighed as she walked the block from the subway station to her building. The last thing she wanted was to spend the evening with another one of her mother's misguided setups. Her mother had the powers of guilting that had been honed by generations of Indian women.

Nisha had come back from the office only an hour later than her mother had requested. At least she'd get a break from talking and thinking about Sameer. The doorman smiled as she approached the door. "Has he arrived yet?"

By now, even Hector the doorman had learned to recognize her mother's setups. They were always Indian men, well-dressed, and showed up with either a bouquet of flowers if they'd grown up in America or a box of Indian sweets if they had recently immigrated.

Hector nodded and smiled. He opened the door for Nisha, then gave her a broad smile, his blue eyes crinkling jovially. "You might want to give this one a chance. He looks good, and he brought a really nice-looking gift basket."

Hector had been a fixture in her life since they'd moved from India. She remembered the first day they'd arrived at the building. They hadn't reserved the service elevator to move their things in the way they were supposed to. Residents were yelling at them for using the regular elevator. Nisha was trying mightily to make do with a walker rather than the wheelchair. Hector had been the only kind soul who had helped them figure it all out. He worked fewer shifts now, his age making it difficult to stand for hours at a time. Nisha had lobbied the co-op board to allow him a chair; after a tough battle, she'd finally won.

"You say that about every guy she invites over."

"I want to see you settled and happy, m'girl," he said. If it had been any other man, she would've lectured him on the fact that she didn't need a man to feel settled and happy but she knew that Hector meant well. Just like her mother. She gave him a kiss on the cheek and made her way to the apartment.

Nisha leaned against the elevator wall as the ancient machine slowly lumbered up to the nineteenth floor. *Sameer is back.* She hadn't allowed herself to think about what that really meant in the flurry to get contracts finalized. Nisha was both excited and scared. There were thousands of designers who would kill for the break she had; Jessica was right. She couldn't throw it away. She had to ignore Sameer; pretend he hadn't come back. Maybe she should think more seriously about Aidan, the Wall Street guy whose company had declined to invest in her business. He'd taken her out for an apology dinner. Since then, they'd seen each other once or twice a month. He wanted to see more of her but she'd resisted. Aidan was intelligent and nice, but something was missing. Maybe it was that he was too *American* for her. He was a steak-and-potatoes type of guy and she was a vegetable-biryani-and-mango-lassi type of woman. Even though she'd moved to New York seven years ago, she still felt out of place. Aidan often brought up cultural references that were totally foreign to her.

Maybe I should give Ma's Indian setups a chance. It wasn't as if she was doing much better on her own. The last setup guy had been really nice, an interventional cardiologist with a good sense of humor. If only he hadn't thought that fashion design was a hobby that she dabbled in while she waited to get married and have babies. Marriage wasn't what she was ready for but it was a recurring theme among her mother's setups. They had agreed to be set up by their own mothers because they were ready to settle down. She wasn't—a fact her mother didn't accept. What she needed was a part-time boyfriend. A man she enjoyed spending time with when she needed a break from work, and was readily available for business dinners and society events where bringing a date was necessary. Aidan was great for stuff like that, which was why she'd kept him around.

The elevator dinged open and she braced herself as she walked down the carpeted floor to her door. She'd barely inserted her key in the lock when her mother pulled the door open. "Nisha, I've been waiting for you, darling. You won't believe who's here."

Nisha sighed. Her mother always made a theatrical display of how they had unexpected company, which was why she was deliberately late coming home from work and hadn't bothered to dress for dinner or put on a fresh coat of lipstick. She knew it was her mother's way of making sure her guest didn't detect Nisha's apathy.

But before Nisha had a chance to say anything, a voice came from the living room and sent an ice pick right through her heart.

"Auntie, Nisha just got home. Give her some time to decompress. I'm in no rush."

Sameer!

How dare he show up here? How had her mother let him in? If there was one person who understood what Nisha had gone through when Sameer broke her heart, it was her mother. It was her mother who had cared for her after the accident, washed her hair, changed dirty bedsheets when she hadn't made it to the bathroom, and held her when she cried in pain. The woman had suffered every surgery and doctor's visit alongside Nisha.

She refused to look in Sameer's direction but turned to her mother. "Ma! How could you?"

Her mother put a finger to her lips, then said unnecessarily loudly, "Yes, let me help you with the zipper in your bedroom." She pulled Nisha down the short hallway and shoved her into the bedroom, kicking the door with her foot.

"Nisha, don't be rude," her mother whispered.

"Ma, how could you invite him here! After everything he's done."

"Nisha, lower your voice. He's a guest in our home, and don't forget our families have been friends for decades."

"I don't care. We are no longer friends."

Her mother looked away.

"Wait, have you kept in touch with them?"

"So what? His mother was my best friend. Did you expect me to cut off all ties just like that?"

"Aren't you the one who used to curse Sameer every time I had to go into surgery? Every time I woke up at night because the pain was so bad? How could you forget all that?"

"Nisha, you yourself said that the accident was not Sameer's fault."

"He broke my heart."

"You both were so young. What did you know of love? Now you're both older, more sensible."

"He hasn't changed, Ma. Have you seen his Instagram account? While I was getting surgery after surgery, he was out having a good time. Girls were commenting on how sexy he was at this party and that. Did he call me once to see how I was? No. He was too busy…"

"I was busy being selfish."

Nisha's face grew hot as she turned toward the door and noticed that it had swung open. Sameer was standing on the other side wearing jeans and a white polo shirt. His hair was styled back but a lock stubbornly fell across his forehead. *Damn him!* He looked so heartbreakingly handsome, with large puppy-dog eyes and kissable pink lips. Nisha found it hard to focus on the anger that was burning through her.

"Sameer, *beta*, don't mind Nisha. She is surprised to see you. Please don't be bothered by her bad behavior."

"Ma, you are not to…"

"Auntie, Nisha absolutely should be angry at me. Please, may I have a chance to explain?"

Nisha began to tell him he could go to hell but Sameer spoke over her. "We were friends for a long time. For the sake of that past friendship, won't you at least give me a chance to talk?"

Her mother squeezed her arm. "Dinner is already on the table. Why don't we go eat and talk."

Nisha stepped away from her mother. "I'm not hungry." She made a show of looking at her watch, then glared at Sameer. "You have three minutes to say what you want to say."

"Nisha!" Her mother went to stand between her and Sameer to block Nisha from closing the door but she wasn't going to be deterred. Sameer had wormed his way into her business. She wasn't going to let him into her home life as well. She'd deal with her mother later. She locked eyes with Sameer and tapped her watch.

"Look, I was a terrible person. I was so caught up in myself that I didn't for a second think about you or anyone else. And for that I'm sorry."

Good start.

"I'd had too much to drink that night and I never should have driven you. I was young and stupid and I risked your life. I had no idea how much you went through after the accident. I thought about you, I wanted to get in touch with you, but once I got out of the hospital, you and your mum had already moved to New York and my mother said it was best I didn't contact you. You're right about the Instagram photos. I hated myself and kept going down a self-destructive path. But…"

"…but now you've changed. You've realized the error of your ways and you're trying to make things right. Is that it?"

His face fell and the pain that flashed in his eyes gave her pause. It was a low blow. He had suffered too. But then she shifted on her feet and felt the pain in her leg that was a permanent part of her life. He still didn't get it and he didn't deserve any consideration from her.

"You haven't changed a bit, Sameer. You are still the selfish person you always were. You're here to make yourself feel better."

"That's not true, Nisha. I'm here for you," he said softly.

"If that's really true, Sameer, then ask me what I need." Her voice had a bite to it.

Time stood still as he gazed at her pleadingly. The anger fueling her started to fizzle out. "What do you need from me?" he asked in a voice that was so small, it caught a string in her heart and tugged.

She steeled herself. It was too easy to fall prey to his charms. "I need you to leave me alone, Sameer. Don't interfere in my business, don't show up at my house. Let me be. Forget we ever knew each other. Can you do that?"

"Nisha!" her mother screamed but Nisha held up a hand.

"I'll try my best, Nisha." And with that, he turned around and left.

Four

It had been a month since they'd officially signed the papers to partner with the Mahal Group. As a newcomer to Fashion Week, it wasn't easy to get listed on the official list of designers. Arjun, Sameer's older brother and head of the Mahal Group, had called in a favor to make sure Nisha made it into the listing. Seeing *Nisha*, the name of her label, listed on the website had been unreal.

Nisha was in her office with Jessica going over the impossibly long list of tasks they had to get through. Jessica had been stressing about the guest list but she needn't have worried. They were getting requests for invitations faster than they could process them, including from social media influencers, major department store buyers and top stylists. Arjun had strategically secured them one of the first spots on the Fashion Week schedule. Technically their show was the Friday before Fashion Week but if they got the right coverage, other new designers would be compared with her rather than the other way around.

It had been a ridiculously busy month. Even with Jessica handling the business side of things, Nisha had to figure out which designs she could have ready for the lookbook and whether they could handle some exclusive drops. She shouldn't have had even a second to think about Sameer, and yet she expected to see him every time they had a Zoom meeting with the Mahal Group. When only Vinod appeared on the screen, instead of relief, annoyance spread through her. She longed to ask where Sameer was, yet managed to keep her mouth shut. Jessica had attended the one in-person meeting they'd had but she reported that Sameer hadn't shown up to that either.

"I heard from Vinod that Sameer is back in town," Jessica said cheekily. "Maybe he'll be at the site visit today."

Nisha's heart gave an extra thump but she ignored it. "It makes no difference to me whether he's there or not," she said haughtily.

Jessica gave her a skeptical look but didn't press the issue. Nisha felt guilty for not opening up to her. She had never been more grateful than now for Jessica's friendship and her business sense. In the last month, Jessica had worked day and night so Nisha could focus on getting the clothes ready. When Nisha had first convinced Jessica to leave her job, she figured that she'd be able to match Jessica's former salary in six months. It had been more than a year since that day and Jessica was making a fraction of her former salary but she hadn't mentioned it once.

"Well, I have to say that when I asked him to be a silent partner, he was really gracious about it. He said something to the effect that he just wanted to see you succeed and if the best way to do that was to stay out of your way, then he was happy to do it."

That should have made Nisha feel better but it didn't. She needed Sameer to be the asshole that she'd angered over for the last several years so she could validate the time she'd spent hating him.

"I'm sure if he shows up today, he'll gleefully rub in the fact that we couldn't find another location."

Jessica shook her head. "You didn't have to be so rude to him at your house. Even though we went with the hotel because we couldn't find another venue, he was right about the fact that the exclusivity made the A-listers want to come even more."

Nisha rolled her eyes.

"Soooo… When are you going to make up with your mother? Not that I mind you as a guest, but you're going to need your sleep and I know how lumpy my couch is."

Nisha sighed. The night Sameer had shown up to her house, she'd had a huge fight with her mother after he left. Her mother felt that Nisha's unyielding attitude toward Sameer was unnecessarily harsh. Especially since he'd apologized. How did she explain to her mother that even after all these years, he was apologizing for the wrong thing? He still didn't understand how badly he'd broken her heart. All her mother knew is that she and Sameer had a falling-out, but Nisha hadn't given her all the details. While she was close to her mother, she still couldn't bring herself to admit that she'd lost her virginity to Sameer.

All these years she'd assumed her mother had lost touch with Sameer's family because unlike Nisha, her mother blamed him for the accident. But her mother had admitted that she had reconnected with Sameer's mother. Apparently now that Arjun had expanded the family hotels to the US, Sameer's parents regularly visited Las Vegas and New York to see their granddaughter. On one such visit, Sameer's mother had gotten in touch with her mother and they'd made up over Turkish afternoon tea at the Baccarat Hotel. Nisha now suspected that her mother was responsible for the Mahal Group investing in her fashion label.

She'd walked out the night Sameer had come to her home and gone to Jessica's apartment. She'd been back home just once to pick up clothes and essentials. Her mother had given her the silent treatment and Nisha returned it in kind. She knew that if she hoped to make up with her mother, she'd have to apologize, and she was in no mood to do that. Her mother had gone too far this time.

"Let's get our label launched and then maybe I can afford a place of my own," Nisha said.

Jessica shook her head. "You're going to give up that primo condo for a roach-infested studio? Hey, why don't you take my place and I'll move in with your mum. She cooks, she cleans, she does errands, and when you're feeling down, she makes you that amazing cup of chai."

Nisha sighed guiltily. Her mother did take really good care of her, and all her efforts had allowed Nisha the freedom to spend her time focusing on business. How could she forget, even for a moment, how much her mother had sacrificed for her? She'd given up her home, her marriage, her whole life for Nisha's sake. "I'll go home tonight."

Jessica smiled. "Let's get going. I'm calling an Uber for our ride to the site visit. I don't want to show up there smelling like subway pee. By the way, your lipstick is looking a little bitten. You might want to freshen your face, you know, just in case."

Nisha threw a pen in her direction, purposely missing. Once Jessica had left, she opened her compact mirror and touched up her makeup. There was absolutely no reason not to look fabulous, and it had nothing to do with whether or not Sameer would possibly be there.

Nisha hadn't been to the new Mahal hotel in Manhattan. She hadn't even known that Sameer's family had bought it. She'd known the old owners, Rajiv and Gauri. They were family friends. She had even attended their wedding in India. That was in the old days, back before the accident, when each weekend was filled with social events among India's elite. When they'd first moved to New York, she knew Rajiv had helped her mother find the condo they eventually bought. Those days were a haze of physical therapy appointments, fashion design courses and interning for other fashion houses to get experience. When had Rajiv and Gauri sold the hotel? Why had they sold it? She realized that when she left Sameer and India behind, she'd left all of her friends as well.

She bit her lip as she entered the hotel. She vaguely remembered coming to the opening when Rajiv had bought it. There were some significant changes. Whereas Rajiv had preferred a New York chic style, the hotel had been transformed into what she pictured an old Rajasthani palace would look like. It reminded her a lot of Sameer's home in India, which was an actual former palace. The high-ceilinged lobby had intricate moldings in shades of dark blue and gold. Delicate Swarovski crystal chandeliers hung from the ceiling. The tiled floor was patterned in a pleasing mandala design that added just the right touch of ethnic glamour. Nisha had read an article about Arjun's wife, Rani, who was an interior architect. She'd bet that Rani had designed this place and appreciated the elegant artistry. It's what she aspired to in her own work, bringing the beauty of India into Western style.

Vinod met them in the lobby. Sameer was nowhere to be seen. Vinod directed them to the ballroom where they were having the show.

Nisha's heart sank when she saw the ballroom. It was an elegant space with a royal-blue-and-gold carpet and high ceilings. But the problem was clear as soon as they walked in. When they'd seen the room specifications, the diagram hadn't shown two poles that cut up the room. They'd have to place the catwalk off-center, which would limit the seating area.

She looked at Jessica, whose pinched expression indicated she had come to a similar conclusion. "How are we going to fit in the confirmed attendees?"

"We're going to open those back doors, put up a tent and allow some of the B-list guests to sit there."

She whirled when she heard Sameer's voice. He walked toward them, dressed in a perfectly cut black business suit with a crisp white shirt that was open at the neck. No tie. He never wore ties. Her pulse jumped as he neared and she smelled his cologne. It was the same one he'd always worn, a slightly spicy but subtle scent that was irresistibly sexy.

"September can be unpredictably cool in New York. You don't have enough land outside for space heaters," Nisha fired back.

"You let us worry about figuring out that technicality."

"You should've let us know about these poles when we first expressed reservations about this space." Nisha shook her head, seething inside. It was just like Sameer to gloss over the things that didn't work in his favor. "This won't work. We'll have to find another location."

Jessica touched her arm. "Nisha, I've exhausted all possibilities. We can't afford another location. Plus, all the event details have already gone out."

"Then we cancel the show, wait until February and work on finding a proper location."

"I suppose, but you're going to have to redesign your entire collection. You've been working on that for a year with a fall show in mind. I guess if we…"

Jessica was wavering; Nisha knew she could convince her to wait. They had to get this show right.

"It's not going to be any better in February. You've got to learn to compromise," Sameer cut in.

Nisha glared at him. "I thought you were going to be a silent partner."

He shook his head. "Not anymore."

Her heart skipped a beat. "Excuse me?"

He stepped forward. "Someone needs to save you from yourself. Your collection is perfect, seven of the top hitters in fashion and social media have already committed to coming. You don't have the finances to wait until February. Trust me, we will make this ballroom work."

So, Sameer had been silently following the updates they'd sent to Vinod.

"Even if we only seat some of the A-listers, your show will be a success."

"What if only a few show up and they all hate

it? Then what? I need to have a wide audience. Not just social media influencers, I need stylists, buyers, magazine editors. I need to cast a wide net. You don't understand what's at stake here."

His face softened. "Your designs are incredible, Nisha. I know you're worried but trust me, I'll make this happen for you."

Traitorous tears stung her eyes. There was a lot riding on this show. Her mother had staked her entire life on her, and Nisha had no other plan if her label failed. But what did Sameer know of all that? He'd had chance after chance handed to him. He had a supportive family, a brother and sisters who took up the mantle when he failed. Nisha only had herself and her mother to rely on. Her mother had given up her home, her marriage, everything. The money her mother had gotten from her father was running out. There was little time left for Nisha to make the label a success and support herself and her mother.

"I wouldn't trust you to keep my cactus alive."

"Probably a good decision, you know I have a black thumb."

She blew out a sigh of frustration. "See, this is why I can't work with you. You can't be serious for a second. Everything is a joke to you." She took a breath to stem the tide of anger that threatened to overtake her. "I... My company is not one of those projects that you use to entertain yourself and then discard when you get bored. It's my livelihood."

I am not going to let you throw me away again.

She tamped down on the thought. This was not about her. It was about her company. It was a business decision. He didn't know the fashion industry. *Neither do I.* She bit her lip to keep her inner critic from overtaking her.

"May we talk privately?" he asked in an even tone.

Nisha was about to refuse, then realized how childish that would seem. She lifted her chin. "If we must."

Sameer nodded to Vinod, who moved toward Jessica. He touched Nisha's elbow and she pulled her arm away. He clenched his teeth, then gestured for her to follow him down the hallway and to the elevator. She assumed they were going to the hotel offices but she startled when he pressed the button for the penthouse.

"Where are we going?"

"To the family apartments. Arjun had the top-floor suites redesigned so whichever family member was based here or visiting had a place to call home."

She swallowed. Going up to a cozy hotel room with Sameer was a terrible idea.

"Don't worry, it's not a hotel room, it's more like a small palace up there."

She hated how her emotions showed on her face. "I can handle myself, thank you very much." She injected as much venom into her voice as she could manage.

He stepped closer to her. She resisted the compulsion to step away. He leaned down and his breath caressed her ear. A shiver ran down her spine but she forced herself to keep absolutely still, watching the numbers, wishing the elevator could go faster up the eighty-some levels in the hotel.

"It's good for one of us to have some control," he whispered. The warmth of his breath, the scent of his woodsy cologne, the heat from his body was too much. She shifted and then mercifully the elevator dinged, indicating they were at their destination.

Sameer extended his arm, blocking the elevator door from closing as she stepped directly into the penthouse suite. Sameer was right. The place was far from a romantic hotel room. With an entire wall made of glass showing a spectacular view of Times Square and Midtown, the space was palatial. There was an open kitchen, a living room, a dining room and a spiral staircase the led up to another floor. A tiled fireplace soared to the ceiling. There was no mantel but the fireplace held a painted family portrait that showed Sameer's parents, his brother Arjun and wife Rani, their sister Divya, Arjun's young daughter, and Sameer's younger sisters, Karishma and Naina. Nisha's mother had shown her the magazine articles about Divya. Nisha was bowled over when she learned that Divya had become a singer, with a hit album no less. When Nisha knew Divya, she had been so serious about her law studies. More than that, she couldn't imagine Sameer's mother approving of a career like that for her daughter. Nisha had spent some time with

Divya and had always liked Sameer's sister. She was happy that Divya had pursued her dreams.

"So who else is here from your family?" A lump formed in her throat as she stared at the picture. When she was in college, an older version of the same portrait had hung in their Rajasthan home and Nisha had imagined herself standing next to Sameer.

"Just me right now. My parents and Arjun are in Vegas. Divya is off jetting somewhere with her fiancé and soon-to-be husband, Ethan."

"Ethan? He's American?" Nisha was shocked.

Sameer grinned. "Yeah, there's been a lot of change in my family. My parents aren't the same *kah diya na, bas!* type."

Nisha couldn't help smiling at Sameer's reference to the Bollywood movie *Kabhi Khushi Kabhie Gham*, K3G as it was colloquially known, where a dictatorial father lorded over his family, and ended conversations with the Hindi version of *because I said so*. Nisha and Sameer had watched the movie at least ten times together, laughing at how similar the dad in that movie was to their own domineering fathers. Sameer had been the only one she could ever talk to about her parents' complicated relationship, and about the effect it had on her. He'd been the only one to understand her desperation to get out, the one she always went to when she needed a friend.

Tears stung her eyes and she tried to blink them away but that only made it worse.

"Hey, Nisha, what is it?" Sameer was in front of her. He tipped her chin with his hand and bent his head so he could look right into her eyes.

She stepped back from him, unable to take his touch and the natural familiarity between them.

"Nisha, we were friends once. Can you find a way to forgive me for the accident?"

Her chest ached every time he apologized for the accident. How could he be so clueless? There was a time when he knew her every thought and wish, when he could finish her sentences. "You keep apologizing for the wrong thing."

He frowned, confusion etched on his handsome face.

"I don't blame you for the accident. The other driver was drunk and came into our lane. You veering off the road when you did probably saved our lives. I was wasted. It might have been worse if I'd driven myself home."

"Or it might not have happened if I'd put you in a taxi with a driver who hadn't had anything to drink." He took a step toward her. "And I should have done a better job finding you after I got out of the hospital and apologized a lot sooner."

She sighed. He really didn't know? "I don't blame you for the accident," she repeated. "I blame you for breaking my heart. We were friends for more years than I can count, you were the love of my life and when we finally had sex, you treated me like one of your cheap one-night stands." The words that had been stuck in her throat since she'd seen him a month ago tumbled out of her.

He took a step toward her but she backed away. It was time they had it out, said what needed to be aired.

"How could you ever think that? You're the one who wanted to make love that night. Remember, I tried to stop you."

"So what? I forced you?"

"No, of course not. I only meant that it wasn't my intention to sleep with you that night. Our friendship was important to me. I didn't want to disrespect you, to ruin our friendship."

"So you broke up with me the next day?" she said incredulously.

"Because we made a mistake."

"You made a mistake."

He ran his hand through his hair, then grabbed a fistful of it. Her breath caught as she recognized the gesture. He used to do that when he didn't understand something, like a complicated calculus problem. When they sat for their national board exams, she would sneak looks at him to see how he was doing and could tell by how much he was pulling his hair how vexed he was.

"You came to me that night upset and distraught over what your father had done. You were vulnerable and in a state. I should have been stronger. I was trying to do the right thing by ending things between us. You know how I was back then, what a mess I was. I didn't want to hurt you and I thought you regretted that night too."

"What made you think I regretted it?"

"When I was driving you home that night, you said that we'd been careless, that we should have controlled ourselves."

"I meant we should have used protection."

He stared at her, then turned around, and while she couldn't see his face, she knew he was rubbing his temple. She stared at his back. *Is he really that stupid?* "Is that why you broke up with me? You thought I had regrets?" It couldn't be. They'd been best friends. He knew that she was in love with him. How often had she brought up the idea that when they graduated, her parents could go to his family to arrange their *rishta*?

Rishta. The word meant so much more than just relationship. It was a promise—between two people, between two families. Their night together was supposed to be the culmination of their friendship and the start of their life together as lovers and then life partners. How could he think that she would give him her virginity and then think it was a mistake? He wasn't very good at relationships but even he wasn't that socially inept.

She took a breath. "Look, if we're going to make this business relationship work, we need to be honest with each other. Even if you thought I'd regretted us having sex, you know there is no way I wanted our relationship to end. So, what was really going on?"

He remained with his back turned to her. She gave him a minute to collect his thoughts but when the silence stretched beyond her tolerance, she stepped around until she was facing him. "You came back into my life. You're the one who wants to be a not-so-silent partner in my business." She hated the high pitch and volume of her voice but she was fast losing control of the hurricane of emotions storming through her. All of the anger, frustration and pain she'd bottled up to move on with her life threatened to explode out of her and she didn't care. It was time for Sameer to face her.

"I'm trying to find the right words here. I don't want to say the wrong thing."

"Start with why you told me we shouldn't see each other the night of the accident."

"Because I knew you loved me in a way that I couldn't return."

There it is. What she'd known all these years. What she'd known the night she'd begged him to make love to her. She'd felt him slipping from her and figured that if they made love, he'd be hers forever. How foolish she'd been.

"I knew you wanted to get married and start a life together but I wasn't there, Nisha. Not with you, not with anyone. I was attracted to you, what man wouldn't be, but I didn't feel the same way you did. I shouldn't have made love to you and I knew it. At the time I couldn't resist and I hated myself for it as I drove you home that night. I realized that it was your first time, I knew what it would mean to you and I didn't want things to get too far out of hand. So when you said we should have controlled ourselves, I was so relieved that I thought maybe you regretted it too. When we met up at the bar the next day, you looked so beautiful that all I could think about was the night before so I knew I had to end it right away, before things got to the point where we wouldn't be able to go back."

Her breath was stuck in her throat and her chest hurt so much that she couldn't move, couldn't talk, couldn't say a word.

Sameer's eyes met hers, pleading. What was she supposed to do? Berate him for not loving her back? Slap him for taking her virginity when she'd practically begged him to? The rational side of her knew there was nothing more to say or do. He hadn't said anything she didn't already know but she'd needed to hear him say the words. Needed to have him acknowledge out loud that he'd never loved her the way she had loved him.

He placed his hands on her shoulders and she stepped away, slapping his hands away. "You don't get to touch me. You don't get to be my friend. If I had my way, you would never get to see my face ever again."

Five

Sameer took a deep breath. *I deserve her hatred.* He held up his hands, taking a step back from her. "You're right. I don't deserve your forgiveness. I was and still am a total jackass. But just hear me out on what I should have said that night."

He paused, waiting for her to walk away, but when she stood with her arms crossed, he went on. "You know I never took college seriously enough. You're the one who pushed me to study. If it weren't for you, I probably wouldn't have even made it to the board exams. But that night we had sex, I'd gotten a call from the college principal. He said he wasn't going to let me graduate. My marks just weren't good enough and I failed two of the final exams."

Her face softened just a touch.

"I was feeling miserable. Then you showed up and your day had been even worse. I needed you and you wanted to be with me and I wasn't thinking. It felt good—no, it was amazing to be with you."

Her lips thinned. "You used me for comfort."

He didn't dare step toward her, even though he wanted to touch her. To somehow make her understand what he was feeling because words were clearly not cutting it. If she were any other girl, he would've placated her with the words he knew she wanted to hear. *Of course it wasn't comfort. I loved you. I wanted to be with you. I just got scared that we'd taken a step that would put me in a place I didn't want to be.*

"It wasn't just comfort," he said.

Her lips pressed together and she turned her gaze away from him. He knew that look. She was pissed. Really pissed. So much so that she didn't even have the words to yell at him.

"Have I mentioned that I was—no, I am an ass?" He smiled, hoping it would have the effect it used to have on her, but her face remained stony.

"I can't forgive you," she said quietly.

Her words knocked the wind out of him. When he'd first learned he would be working with Nisha, he knew she'd be mad at him but he assumed that they could get past it. Now he wasn't so sure. He blew out a sigh of frustration. They had to find a way to make it work. After their last meeting, he'd given her the space she'd requested but Vinod had called him two days ago to say that their business financials were in rough shape. Nisha had overspent on the production of her line. Apparently, labor costs for embroidery had skyrocketed from the initial estimates she'd been given. Global supply chain issues also meant that she'd overspent on fabrics and other raw materials. Sameer couldn't let his brother, Arjun, find out that the one thing he'd entrusted to Sameer was falling apart. This was a test for Sameer, a way for him to prove to himself more so than his family that he was ready to be the man he wanted to be.

He also needed to make things right with Nisha by making her label a success. But if she didn't go through with the fashion show and start selling, not only would the Mahal Group lose its investment, her business would be bankrupt in a month.

This was his first challenge. He'd begged for forgiveness, and he'd tried to reason with her. What more could he do? There was only one way forward, one he didn't want to take but she'd left him with no choice.

He hardened his voice and his heart. "You don't have to forgive me, but you do need to recognize that you have a serious cash flow problem and if you don't do this show, you won't last until February. I'm a major investor in your business and we have a contract."

He barely caught the flicker of pain in her eyes

before her face turned to stone. "I knew this was a mistake from the beginning. To hell with the contract."

She turned away from him.

"Fine, we can shred the contract. All you have to do is fire all your staff, and cut us a check for the original investment plus interest."

She froze and he knew he had her. She might have grown up some but the college girl he knew cared more about the people in her life than she did about herself. There was no way she would ruin other people's lives for her pride.

He positioned himself in front of her. "Look, the entire idea of the Mahal hotels investing in your business was to help you succeed. You are the first investment we've made to see if the program will work. We don't have to be friends but we do need to work together."

She looked up at him with narrowed eyes and his chest tightened. It wasn't just anger she was feeling toward him. She didn't believe that he was on her side. It was written plain as day on her face.

"You forget that I know the way your brother works. How many times did you tell me that Arjun is all about the bottom line and cutting losses. This might be a teeny-tiny investment to your family, but this is my life's work."

Sameer ran his fingers through his hair, resisting the urge to literally pull it out. *How do I get through to her?* "Have you read the terms of your contract?"

She rolled her eyes.

"Then you know that if your business tanks, we lose our investment. What you don't know is that your label is the test for a larger program that is near and dear to Rani's and Divya's hearts. Why would I possibly want you to fail? Do you think I want to face my brother, my sister-in-law and my sister and have to tell them that I screwed up? Again?"

Her face softened. She was the only person he had talked to about how he felt growing up in his brother's shadow. He took a step toward her and she didn't move.

"Look, I don't know the first thing about fashion, but I know how to launch a business. Your show has some great social media influencers coming. If we seat just ten to twelve of the right people around the catwalk and they post pictures of your show, the press buzz will have orders coming in."

"What if the A-listers don't come, or worse, they hate it? I don't want to pin the success of this show on just a few people."

He finally heard it. The fear in her voice. That's what her resistance was about.

He stepped close and placed his hands on her shoulders. She tensed but didn't move away. "Look at me." She looked up. *How did I miss it?* The pressure, the fear, the stress was written all over her face.

"Your talent is amazing. There aren't many thirty-year-old designers launching their own labels and having a show during Fashion Week. You are not alone. There is a whole team behind you. Jessica, Vinod…me."

She nodded and stepped back. "There's a lot to do and not a lot of time to do it."

They went back to the ballroom, where Vinod introduced her to Rose, a petite strawberry blonde who was the hotel's event coordinator. Nisha liked her immediately.

"I've done two fashion shows at other hotels. I know what the vibe needs to be." She walked Nisha and Jessica through where the catwalk would be located and how the seats would be positioned. Nisha noticed that Sameer was leaving the ballroom. She missed him when he wasn't around but his presence put her on edge. Their talk had helped but it hadn't resolved anything between them. It was just a temporary cease-fire to get through her show.

"Let's go to the restaurant and talk food and drink."

Rose led them to a small private room in the hotel restaurant. There were only four of them but the table was set for five. Was Sameer coming or was that just the standard table size in this private space?

"Since your line is all about Eastern-inspired Western style, we've come up with some fusion items for the food that'll be served to the guests."

A waiter appeared with five champagne glasses

filled with a golden, bubbly drink. Her eyes went to the door but there was no Sameer.

"This will be our signature cocktail that we will call the Golden Nisha. It's prosecco with a touch of turmeric, ginger and cinnamon." Rose held up her glass and they all clinked glasses. The waiter set the extra glass at the empty seat next to Nisha.

"Yum!" Jessica exclaimed and Nisha had to agree. The flavors reminded her of chai and went perfectly with the sweet prosecco.

"This is such a great idea."

"I'd love to take credit but Sameer came up with the idea for the drink. Wait until you taste the food."

She couldn't help it. The mention of his name made her pulse jump. He'd been working in the background on the food for her show? Who was this guy? She eyed the untouched cocktail next to her.

"While we wait for the food, let's talk swag bags. What are you guys thinking?"

Jessica answered. "We've been working with this group in India that supports small women's businesses in rural areas. We've purchased various pieces of handmade jewelry, and we'll include shawls embroidered with Nisha's designs."

"I love that," said Rose.

"Do you have the bags you're going to put them in?"

Nisha turned to see Sameer walking into the room. He took the empty seat next to her and her entire body warmed. *Dammit*. Why did he have that effect on her? How could she still be attracted to him after everything that had happened? After the conversation she'd just had with him? He'd used her for comfort. *Comfort*. What the hell was that? How could he use her that way? Especially after she'd confided in him about what had happened with her father. She hadn't known about him failing out of college. That made things even worse. He wasn't comforting her; he had comforted himself.

"Nisha?"

She'd lost track of the conversation. "I'm sorry, what was the question?"

"Sameer was just suggesting custom-made gift bags that are co-branded with the Mahal hotel," Jessica summarized.

Was that his new angle? Was he using her fashion show to promote his family business?

"I only bring up that idea because if the Mahal name goes on the bag, we can pay for them. Our name can be small."

"That's a great deal," Jessica chimed in.

Nisha nodded, unable to trust herself to speak. Her mind was a tornado of mixed emotions and thoughts. He'd come up with food for her event, and he was trying to find a way to pay for things. Since when did he think about things like swag bags?

A waiter appeared with a tray. "So we're going to serve finger foods on passed trays. We have pumpkin samosas, chicken tikka Wellington, cocktail shrimp masala, naan pizza bites and a rose jalebi for something sweet."

Nisha stared at the food on her plate and looked at Sameer. Did he remember? "I got the idea for the pizza bites from that time in the hostel."

She smiled. He did remember.

"What's this now?" Rose asked.

Sameer grinned at Nisha and her heart jumped. "When Sameer and I were in college, there was this one night when we stayed up late studying. We were craving pizza but everything was closed so we looked through the common kitchen and all we found was some naan, onions, tomatoes and paneer. So we came up with this idea of smashing the tomato for sauce, using the paneer as cheese and the naan as the crust and made a pizza in the microwave. It sounds terrible but it ended up being really good."

She popped the pizza naan in her mouth and moaned. "Okay, this is heaven."

As she turned toward him, she caught the smoldering look in his eyes. Her face warmed. "I'm so glad you like it," he said, his voice thick.

Jessica cleared her throat. "Well, I can't thank you enough for thinking through all these details. All of these items are to die for. Compliments to your chef."

"You can thank him right now." Rose gestured to Sameer.

Nisha turned to him. "You cook?"

He shrugged. "It's a new hobby, and Rose is exaggerating. I came up with the ideas. The chefs here made it happen."

Sameer cooking? Being modest? Who was this man?

"When did you take up cooking?" The man she knew liked to eat but other than the one time they had cooked together, she had never seen him even make chai.

"Arjun loves cooking. He said it was stress relieving for him. In fact, he impressed my sister-in-law, Rani, by cooking for her on one of their first dates."

Rose put a hand on her heart. "That's so cute. I can't imagine Arjun in anything other than a business suit giving orders."

Nisha, Sameer and Vinod laughed. Vinod, who had been quiet the whole time, spoke up. "The first time I met Mr. Singh, I was so nervous, I was sweating like crazy. After he interviewed me, he told me that if I want to work for him, I have to find a better deodorant, get nicer clothes and speak more confidently."

They all laughed.

"So Arjun hasn't changed?" Nisha asked.

Sameer smiled. "When it comes to business, he's the same. But Rani has changed him. He's different at home, more supportive, less like a dictator."

"Remember that time he confiscated the video game?" Nisha smiled at the memory.

Sameer made a face. Nisha turned to the rest of the group. "There was a party at Sameer's house and I was there with my family. We were in secondary school and were bored out of our minds. So we decided to sneak out to his room and play video games. There were like a hundred people there. Who would miss us? We were playing *Duke Nukem* and we were in this intense level and Arjun suddenly appears and starts lecturing us on our familial responsibilities. Sameer told Arjun that he couldn't make him do anything so Arjun unplugs the machine and takes it with him."

"Wow, I did not know you and Sameer were so close," Vinod remarked.

Nisha looked at Sameer. They hadn't just been close, they'd been the best of friends. The kind who knew all of each other's hopes, dreams and secrets. She would've done anything for him. Helped him bury a body if he'd asked. But he'd never given her the same importance in his life that she'd given him in hers.

She wiped her mouth on the napkin and set it on the plate. "We were close—" she looked pointedly at Sameer "—once."

Six

Nisha had moved back home three weeks ago. Making up with her mother hadn't been hard. She refused to apologize, and so did her mother, but they made a deal that Nisha would attend a setup dinner of her mother's choosing, without being late. Nisha knew that even if she didn't agree to her mother's terms, Ma would never turn her away, but she didn't want any tension in the house.

She was glad she'd made up with her mother. Other than the fact that Jessica's couch was hard to sleep on, she and Jessica spent so much time at work together, Nisha realized that her friend had no break. It was all *Nisha* all the time. Nisha was getting sick of hearing her own name and almost wished she'd named the label something else.

"The swag bags have arrived," Jessica shouted from outside. Nisha hurried out of her office, eager to see them. Sameer had taken personal responsibility for ordering the bags. Nisha had been skeptical but with everything going on, she hadn't wanted to dump additional responsibility on Jessica or take it on herself. They were just bags.

Jessica was aggressively slicing the tape on one of the cardboard boxes. A month ago, their studio had been just her, Jessica, bolts of fabric and piles of bills. Now over a dozen staff hurried about. Sewing machines hammered away, a couple of models were being fitted for their dresses and a few interns were folding programs. It looked like a real fashion house.

Nisha's breath caught as Jessica pulled out the first bag. She put her hand on a nearby table to steady herself. *Damn him. Damn him to hell and back.*

"These are beautiful. And expensive. He went all out." Jessica held up the bag, examining it from all sides. It was a black brocade sack with a delicate silver pattern that gathered together at the top with a silver rope. *Nisha* was printed across the side of the bag in silver, and in smaller letters beneath *presented by Mahal Hotels.*

"This looks like something you would design."

Nisha's throat was tight. "It is something I designed."

Jessica looked at her quizzically.

"It was the first thing I designed. I sewed it myself and the thing was falling apart at the seams but I was so proud that I brought it to the college canteen to show it off. Sameer took pictures of me with it and posted it on social media with #NishaFashion."

Jessica put the bag down and stepped toward Nisha, enveloping her in a hug. "Oh, hon, you need to forgive him. He's trying really hard, and the more you try to stay angry at him, the more it zaps your emotional energy."

Nisha barely heard her. She was stuck in the memory of that day ten years ago when she'd waltzed into the college canteen and plopped herself down next to Sameer. Things had been so easy between them. She had proudly shown the group of friends sitting at the table the little *potli* she had designed and they burst into laughter. One girl pointed out the seam that was falling apart. Another guy made a snide comment about it being a good thing that her father was rich. Only Sameer had taken the *potli*, admired it and then had her pose with it so he could take pictures. *You should call your company* Nisha.

Jessica touched her arm. "Rose said that the conference room we'll be using as the dressing room is empty this week. Why don't you take the clothes that are ready and go to the hotel. It's a more convenient location for the models to come for fittings anyway."

Nisha nodded. While she loved being in the hub

of activity, they were running out of space. Most of her work was done. Now the seamstresses had to finish stitching and making adjustments. "I'll take the interns and gift bags with me. They can stuff them there."

"And maybe you can thank Sameer in person for this incredibly sweet gesture," Jessica added.

Nisha gave her friend a look. She called a van service and with the help of her staff, she loaded the boxes and clothing racks. The young interns chatted excitedly during the trip. Nisha remembered when she was carefree like them, excited to be part of her first fashion show. It had been at the Taj hotel in Mumbai. She'd been the low-level assistant assigned to fetch drinks for the models, thread for the seamstresses and crawl on the floor to find lost buttons. Her friends joked that she was a *bai*, a maid to the mercurial designer Naeem Khan, but she'd loved every minute of it. Sameer had shown up backstage at the end of the show with a giant bouquet of flowers. Naeem had thought they were for her and was more than a little pissed to find out they were for the girl whose name she hadn't even bothered to learn. He was the only person who had ever taken her aspirations seriously.

Traffic was snarled as usual. Nisha stared out at the clog of cars inching their way up Broadway and took a deep breath. She hadn't seen him in person for three weeks but he'd been in New York. Despite the fact that they were only two miles away from each other at any given time, the distance between them stretched boundlessly. As much as she wanted to, she didn't know how to forgive him.

When they got to the hotel, Rose directed them to a back entrance where she sent staff to help them unload the boxes. Nisha got the interns set up in the conference room that would serve as their backstage dressing area. She checked the clothes and hung them carefully on the rack. Some of the delicate dresses had lost a couple of beads in transit but she sewed them back on. Naeem had been tough on her but she'd taught Nisha a valuable lesson, which was to make sure that she knew how to do every little thing that was required to make clothes. *If there is one thing you remember, it should be this: never rely on anyone but yourself to get things right.* It was a good lesson for life too.

There was no sign of Sameer. Rose had let him know that Nisha was here. When it was past 8:00 p.m., she sent the interns home. They had stuffed the swag bags, made special ones for the models and staff, and had started setting up the dressing tables. Nisha still had hours of work ahead of her. She would personally pack the gifts for the interns and there were a few last alterations and fixes to the dresses.

If she was going to thank Sameer in person, she couldn't wait any longer. She'd have to go to him. She called the front desk from the in-house phone on the wall and asked if they could connect her to

Mr. Singh. The phone rang forever. She'd almost given up when he answered.

"You know they have these things called cell phones? I didn't even know where this damn phone was. I had to follow the ringing." There was laughter in his voice.

"I don't have your current number." There was a time when he was number one on the speed dial of her mobile phone.

"I'm texting it to you right now."

Of course he had her number.

"Did you need something?" he asked.

Suddenly her mouth was dry. "I want to thank you for the gift bags."

"Come up to the penthouse."

Before she could protest, he hung up. Her hands trembled as she placed the phone back into the receiver. It was a mixture of excitement and nervousness.

She went to the bathroom in the lobby and critically eyed her jeans and plain V-neck T-shirt. Work clothes. There was minimal makeup on her face. She touched the scar on top of her eyebrow and powdered it. She took the mascara out of her purse but then put it back. This was not a date. She was not trying to impress him.

Sameer had texted her the special code she needed to get to the penthouse and she punched it in the keypad. As the elevator rose, she practiced the words she was going to say to him.

He was standing on the other side when the elevator doors opened, and seeing him literally took her breath away. He was wearing gray sweatpants and a black T-shirt. His hair was a little mussed like he'd been pulling at it. This is how he'd looked when they lived in the college hostel. It was the look she used to fantasize about, and as if by muscle memory, her body reacted.

He stepped toward her and for a second she thought he might give her a hug but he stopped. He looked down at his clothes. "Sorry, I was just chilling."

Had she been staring at him?

She smiled. "I was just thinking you look exactly the same as you did in college."

He blinked and smiled back at her. "Funny, I was thinking the same thing about you. I like seeing you casual."

They stared at each other for what seemed like forever. She was lost in her memories of a time when things seemed simpler. When the biggest problem in her life was to make sure Sameer passed his next exam, and to get him to see her as more than a friend.

"A rupee for your thoughts," he said.

"I was just thinking about how much easier things were when we were in college. Sometimes I wish we could go back to those times."

He gave her a strange look.

"Why don't you come in." He gestured toward

the couches. Though *couches* was not the right word for the matching rolled-arm sofas with nailhead trim and deep button tufting. The royal blue color paired perfectly with the large silver-gray rug that was the centerpiece of the room. Matching silver trim settees completed the square seating area. Incongruent with the perfectly glamorous furnishings was a hodgepodge collection of electronics on the coffee table. Laptop, cell phone, iPad, notepad, pen and a teacup that looked like it was missing a saucer.

She wasn't going to stay. There was a long list of things to do for the show but she found herself taking a seat.

"Do you want something to drink?"

Do I ever! "Do you have a bottle of wine open?"

He shook his head. "I can order some from room service."

"No, it's okay. I'll just have a glass of water."

He waved his hand. "I was about to order dinner anyway. Why don't I get us some food too? Red or white?"

She didn't really want to wait for room service. She'd come for a quick thank-you. To be polite. They were not friends. She didn't want to hang out with him.

He punched a number on his phone. "Red or white?" he repeated.

"Red."

"The chef makes an amazing *malai kofta*."

She nodded. It was her favorite dish. He ordered *malai kofta*, chicken tikka masala, lamb biryani, rice, yogurt, naan and a bottle of red zinfandel.

"That's enough to feed half the hotel."

He grinned. "I'm pretty hungry and if I remember, you can put away your fair share of food."

"I don't think I've seen Indian food on a room service menu."

"That was Rani's idea. We have the traditional items on the menu as well but the room service revenue went up thirty-six percent once we added the Indian food."

She raised a brow. Sameer had never been interested in anything other than partying. She'd once asked him how many hotels they owned and he had no idea. "You've gotten really involved in the family business."

He took a seat on the settee next to her and she was glad he'd put some physical distance between them. "I'm trying. Arjun needs help and Divya is off jetting around doing her music thing. It's time for me to step up."

So you've finally grown up.

"I came to thank you for the gift bags."

"You're welcome."

"I can't believe you remembered that first *potli* I made."

He picked up his cell phone from the coffee table, clicked through for several seconds, then handed her the phone. She stared at the screen. It was a picture of her when she was young, wearing tight jeans, high heels, big hair, and proudly holding the *potli*. Her chest tightened. She'd deleted every single picture of him that she ever had, including all the ones on her social media pages.

"Why?"

"Why what?"

"Why are you being so sweet? Why the bags? Why the food? Why everything?"

"I owe you one. Actually I owe you several."

She swallowed. That's why he was doing all of this for her. He still felt like he owed her for the accident. All of the nice things he was doing were coming from a place of guilt. *Not a place of love.* She looked away from him.

Silence stretched between them, each lost in their own thoughts. A chime from the elevator alerted him that room service was on their way and he pressed a button on the remote control to give them permission to enter. A tuxedoed waiter wheeled in a cart full of food and set up the meal on the table. Sameer pulled out a chair for her to sit and took a seat across from her. The waiter showed the bottle of wine to Sameer and he deferred to Nisha. She nodded her approval and he poured her a taste. It was a nice smooth wine, slightly dry. It would go well with the Indian food. The waiter filled her glass but when he moved to Sameer, he put a hand over his glass and shook his head.

"You aren't drinking?"

Sameer thanked the waiter and shook his head. Nisha frowned. Sameer used to drink a whole bottle of wine before the party even started. The waiter wheeled the cart out. Once he was gone, Sameer turned to her.

"I just got out of rehab, remember. I'm ten months sober."

Seven

Nisha had just spooned some rice onto her plate and she dropped her cutlery with a clank.

Rehab. When she heard the word *rehab*, she thought about the physical and occupational therapy she had gone through. He meant substance abuse rehabilitation. She didn't know what to say. What did you say? *Congratulations on getting sober? Way to go? Sorry you had a habit but glad you broke it?*

"I guess that's good. You always were a heavy drinker."

"I didn't go to rehab for alcohol, but I do abstain from it because addictions go hand in hand." He put down his fork. "After the accident, I went through a few surgeries. I was in a lot of pain. After each surgery, the pain got worse and the docs gave me pills to manage it. I didn't even realize when I was hooked on the pills and used them for more than just pain. It finally got to the point where my family noticed and sent me to rehab."

She stared at him. "Why didn't you reach out? Tell me all of this?"

He tilted his head. "Why didn't you contact me? That night I came for dinner, your mom told me about all of the surgeries you went through, the physical therapy, the injury to your leg. Why did I hear it from your mom and not from you?"

"Probably the same reason I didn't hear from you. It was too much to deal with all at one time."

He nodded. "I didn't even realize I was addicted. You know how it is in India. If you have money, it's easy to get pharmaceuticals. I just felt like I was constantly in pain. It was only after going to rehab that I realized it wasn't just physical pain I was dealing with."

Her throat closed. She wanted to reach out and hug him, to let him know that she understood exactly what he'd gone through. "To be honest with you, I can see how it happened. If it weren't for my mom, I probably would've gotten addicted too. At some point, she threw away the pain medication and started buying me essential oils, giving me homeopathic medicines, ayurvedic ointments and making me go to physical therapy and yoga. It was mentally and physically exhausting."

"But you didn't take the easy way out by taking pills like I did. You did what you've always done, you worked hard."

"I've never been to rehab like you have but ten months of sobriety is pretty significant." She looked guiltily at the bottle of wine. "I'm sorry I didn't know, I thought you'd meant physio or else I'd never have asked for the wine."

He waved his hand and handed her the basket that contained the naan. "I have to learn to be around alcohol. My family is in the hotel business and nothing gets done without a glass of wine or a tumbler of whiskey. I now understand why so many recovering alcoholics work at a bar. In an odd way it's almost reaffirming of the commitment to stay sober."

"You should've told me this earlier."

He smirked. "I tried. I came to have dinner at your house but you threw me out, remember?"

She did remember and felt guilty now for not hearing him out. She'd made assumptions about him based on the social media posts she'd seen. Sameer hadn't been just partying—though he was doing that too—he'd been drowning his sorrows in his own torturous ways. She'd spent so much time being angry and hurt that she hadn't recognized the typical signs. Whenever his parents got on him about not meeting their expectations, he would go out and party hard, drink a lot, and post scandalous pictures on social media. His family saw it as him immaturely acting out and punishing them but she knew that Sameer was coming from a place of pain. The drinking, the partying was his way of distracting himself from the deep hurt he was feeling. It was easier for him to take his family's anger than their disappointment. She had been the one he came to the morning after one of his party binges and bared his heart. Yet she'd seen all of those social media posts and not once had she thought about the fact that he might have been going through something too.

She raised her water glass. "To new beginnings."

He picked up his water with lemon and clinked it with hers. "Does this mean I've been forgiven?"

"I honestly don't know that I have it in me to ever forgive you for breaking my heart. But you have taken the wind out of the sails of my anger. I guess that's progress."

"I'll take what I can get. How are you feeling about the show?"

She took a sip of wine. "Everything is ready. The clothes have been done in record time, the model fittings are going well, the lookbook is perfect..."

"But you're scared."

Her heart squeezed painfully. He had always been able to know what she was feeling, sometimes even before she did. The ache that had settled deep in her chest surfaced again. This is why she couldn't forgive him. He knew her heart better than she did. So how could he break it like he had?

"There's a lot riding on this show. My mom and I came to New York because I wanted to apprentice with one of the big fashion houses. It affected my parents' relationship. Their marriage is in the worst place it's ever been."

"Is it because she stayed here with you?"

Nisha nodded. "In part. She didn't want to leave me alone. I was still in physical therapy. I told her to go back, but she wouldn't."

"Are you sure it was about you? I mean after what happened that night…"

Tears pricked her eyes. She'd never talked about her parents' relationship with anyone except Sameer and even he didn't know the full story. It was intensely private for her mother, and her family's secret would destroy several lives if it ever came out.

"After the accident, my parents really came together for me. They were there, together as a unit."

Sameer leaned back in his chair and put his hands behind his head. His shirt stretched across his chest. She tried not to stare but she'd spent most of her adolescent and adult life fantasizing about his body. As hard as she'd tried to forget their one night together, she could still feel his solid muscles underneath her hands.

"Nisha?"

She snapped out of it. "I'm sorry, what did you say?"

He leaned forward and her heart beat faster as he reached out and put his hand on hers. His touch was warm and while her mind screamed at her to pull her hand back, the familiarity of his warmth was too tempting. She'd lived with the drama of her parents' relationship day in and day out and she couldn't talk to anyone else about it.

"I was asking about your relationship with your dad."

She sighed. All her life she had been Daddy's little girl. Her mother had been the disciplinarian in the house, and Nisha being the only child, her father doted on her. The night she and Sameer had slept together, she had overheard her father on the phone talking with someone. Her father had his phone on speaker and she'd heard him and his mistress making plans to leave their respective spouses. *Darling, I have to move my money overseas. Otherwise, she will get her claws on it. You know how divorce is these days. We can't be stupid about this. Just give me one more year and I'll throw her out on the streets.*

Nisha had confronted her father and they'd had an ugly fight with her vowing never to talk to him again and him threatening to disown her.

"He was there for me after the accident, through the surgeries and the endless doctors' appointments. He and my mom were a team for a while. That afternoon when I caught him talking to his mistress felt like a bad dream. But once we moved here…" A lump formed in her throat. "…he went back to her."

Hold it together. Don't cry, don't cry.

He stood and came around the table. He knelt down beside her but didn't touch her. "I am so sorry, Nisha."

She looked down into his soft brown eyes and suddenly he wasn't the asshole who had ruined her life. He was her friend. The only person in the world she felt comfortable sharing things that she hadn't dared share with anyone else. The only person with whom she could share her innermost thoughts and not feel judged.

"He admitted everything to my mom. Then in the same breath, he asked her to come back because his mistress had ended the relationship and he wanted my mom back. My mom went back to India but returned to New York after a month."

She shook her head and looked away from him. "She refused to tell me what had happened between them but I found out that she'd made a deal with him. He paid for our New York apartment and she'd keep quiet about his affair to save his reputation in society. Apparently, his mistress is married to a prominent businessman. If their affair came out, my father wouldn't just lose face in society, the other husband could make it difficult for him to do business." Saying the words out loud soured her mouth. But she also felt a weight lift from her chest. "He also invested in the fashion label. The whole time I thought it was because we were a family again but I found out that was part of the deal Ma made with him. She lied to me so I wouldn't hate him."

Sameer hung his head. "I wish I'd known. I am so sorry."

"This show has to be a success. I need to pay

my father back the money he initially put in. I need to throw it back in his face. And I need to be financially independent so my mom doesn't feel beholden to him."

"I'll happily write you a personal check right now to pay him off."

She shook her head. "I need to do this on my own." She looked back at her plate. "I'm sorry but I've lost my appetite."

He nodded and stood. "Me too. Why don't I make us some coffee." He held out his hand and her heart squeezed painfully. They had never been a couple in college but it was common for them to hold hands, or walk arm in arm. It didn't mean anything. Yet it seemed too intimate right now. She hesitated then took his hand and he led her to the couch.

He came back with coffee for them and a blanket for her. She hadn't even realized she was hugging herself until he put the velvety blanket on top of her. He handed her a steaming cup of coffee. She took a sip. It was exactly as she liked it. Double cream and extra sweet.

He took a seat next to her, not quite touching her but close enough that she could smell his cologne. The familiar scent soothed her nerves.

"I need to tell you something, Nisha."

She looked up.

"I didn't know how to broach it with you since we were barely on speaking terms but I think you should know."

She swallowed. *This can't be good.*

"When Divya came up with this idea of us branching out and investing in South Asian artists, a lot of people sent in proposals. I wasn't involved in that part but Divya shared with me that Arjun didn't want to invest in your business. He felt it was the riskiest and she agreed."

"Gee, thanks for the confidence booster."

"Sorry, but that's not the important part. My mother insisted that it had to be you because she'd been talking to your mother."

Nisha had suspected this all along, ever since she'd learned that her mother was still talking to her old friend. It wasn't a coincidence that the Mahal Group had suddenly shown up to bail her out after most investment firms had rejected her.

"There's more. Your New York condo is in your mom's name and it's completely paid off. Your mother tried to put up the condo as collateral for our investment."

Nisha put a hand on her mouth to keep from screaming out. Her mother had asked her to make the same offer to other investors and she'd been horrified. She would not put the only thing her mother had left at risk.

"Don't worry, we firmly refused. Instead, what we…no, what I promised is that I would do everything I could to make sure that your show is a success."

She didn't know whether to slap him or hug him. What right did he have to ride in on his motorcycle to be her savior? Yet if he hadn't promised to help, her mother would have gone to someone who might have taken advantage of her. Nisha's heart swelled even more for her mother.

Sameer locked eyes with her. "I was going to wait until after the show was a success to tell you this but I want open communication between us. No lies or half-truths. I didn't want you finding out from someone else."

She nodded. "Does your family know about my parents' marriage?"

He nodded. "Not from me. Your mother told my mother."

"What about the rest of it?"

"The rest of what?"

"The identity of my father's mistress?"

Sameer shook his head. "Your mother has been weirdly protective of your father. I understand now why that is."

"My father paid for her silence," Nisha said bitterly.

Sameer leaned over to the coffee table and pressed the space bar on his laptop. The screen came to life. He turned it around so she could see it. "I've been running the numbers on *Nisha*. If you sell twenty percent of your collection to two major buyers, you can pay off your father's initial investment and ten percent of what you owe the Mahal Group. If you sell thirty percent of your collection…"

He went on going through the numbers. Jessica

had made similar calculations but this wasn't Jessica's spreadsheet. Sameer had put it together. He'd been sitting here on a Friday night working on her business.

She let him go on for a bit, then stopped him. "I know the numbers. But there's a fair chance that none of the buyers will pick me up, or the reviews will be horrible."

He shook his head. "I sent a sneak peek of the digital lookbook to some fashion bloggers, and one of them emailed me an article that's going online tomorrow."

She put a hand on her mouth. "What is it going to say?"

"See for yourself." He clicked through his email and she held her breath. He turned the screen to show her. The words blurred in front of her and she had to take a deep breath and start reading again.

If there is only one new designer to watch, it's Nisha. Her Indian-inspired designs are not just the quintessential East-meets-West, but hit that sweet spot of runway couture that can be worn on the red carpet or to a glam event.

"Oh my God. *Couture Clan* is publishing this tomorrow? They are, like, *the* fashion blog!" She reread the article to make sure she wasn't dreaming. She'd been so afraid that everyone would hate her work that she'd spent all her time bracing for criticism. She hadn't really allowed herself the space to think about what would happen if it was a success.

He nodded and grinned, looking exactly like he had in college. He held up two hands and without thinking, she gave him a double high five and linked her fingers with his. They stared at each other, frozen in body and time. He tightened his grip ever so slightly and she instinctively squeezed back. As an only child in a loveless marriage, she had grown up lonely. The only bright spots in her childhood had been the times when her and Sameer's families got together. They had coordinated going to the same college and for the first time in her life, she hadn't been alone. He'd been there to cheer her on and celebrate each of her achievements.

"I've missed you."

Had she said the words or had he? There was such a big lump in her throat that she was pretty sure she hadn't spoken.

All of the anger and hostility that she'd held in her body for the past eight years threatened to choke her. She loved Sameer. Always had, always would. Through her anger, through her pain, through her hatred, she'd never stopped loving him.

She couldn't stand it any longer. She leaned toward him and he met her halfway. Their lips crashed together and all at once, she let go of his hands and her fingers were in his hair and his hands were around her waist pulling her closer. All of the energy that had consumed her in the last five years came rushing out. She kissed him hard, using her tongue to plunder his mouth. She pushed her breasts against his solid chest. There was an uncontrollable fire inside her. She didn't just want him, she needed him in the kind of physical way a cracked, dry earth needs water. Her body needed to drink him in, consume every inch of him.

She broke the kiss to lift his shirt. He was saying something but she couldn't really hear him. The feel of his naked chest underneath her fingertips, the sight of his erection stretching against his sweatpants and the heat burning inside her core made her lose her mind. This was not the time for rational thought. All she could think about was how much she needed him.

His hands snaked under her shirt, unhooked her bra and cupped her breasts. It wasn't enough. She took her hands off him only long enough to pull her shirt and bra off and unbuckle her jeans. He didn't miss a beat. His mouth captured one nipple while his hand caressed her breast. She raked her hands down his chest, to his belly, and stroked him through his sweatpants. He was long and hard and she was hot and wet. She couldn't stand it anymore. As soon as he took his mouth off her nipple, she stood and in one move took off her panties and jeans. He shed his sweatpants.

"Nisha, are you sure?"

She didn't hear the question. She didn't want to hear it because the only thing she was sure of was that if she didn't get him inside her, she would explode.

She pushed him back onto the couch and straddled him. She took him in her hand and the last vestiges of her consciousness disappeared when he moaned. She slid him inside her. He felt so full and hard, for a second she couldn't move, couldn't breathe, couldn't do anything other than clench against him.

He leaned forward and the movement sent a ripple of pleasure through her so intense that she cried out. He cupped her breasts and moved infinitesimally inside her, sending shudders through her core. She began rocking against him and he pressed his finger lightly against her clit. Too lightly. Increasing her movements, she pushed his finger more firmly against her sensitive spot. A quick learner, he began rubbing it just the way she wanted and it was too much for her. She arched her back as her body imploded and every muscle inside her tightened. She cried out as the wave of release pulsed through her with the intensity of lava erupting from a volcano.

When her body was finally done liberating itself, she noticed that Sameer had gone soft inside her. He was leaning back against the couch, his eyes closed, clearly spent. His hands were on her hips as if to hold her onto him. She should be filled with regret but it felt more like relief. As if she had just let go of a heavy weight that had been pulling her down. This was what she'd needed all along.

And now that she'd had it, she was finally ready to let go of Sameer.

Eight

Shit, shit, shit. Having sex with Nisha was not in the plans. It was so far beyond the wrong thing to do that it could be a *Jeopardy!* question under the category of "Sameer's worst mistakes." They had just gotten to a place of friendship and reconciliation not two minutes ago. But he'd wanted her more than he'd ever wanted anything in his life. Touching her had unlocked a Pandora's box of emotions inside him. The love he'd hidden from her, the sleepless nights he'd spent in the last month thinking about her, the raw, animalistic attraction he felt toward her. All of that had crashed into him the moment she'd leaned forward with her lips parted.

Then it hit him.

"Dammit! Nisha, I'm so sorry, but we didn't use protection." This was almost exactly the way it had happened last time. Except that time, he'd known she was a virgin so he'd taken charge to make sure he didn't hurt her. Still, it had been the same uncontrollable desire that made him forget the little foil packet he always carried in his wallet. This time, he wasn't even sure if there was a condom in the entire suite. He certainly didn't carry one in his wallet these days. Since he'd gotten out of rehab, he'd avoided getting involved with anyone. His psychologist had specifically warned him to take time to focus on himself and not get involved in a relationship. He'd been tested in rehab so he wasn't worried about passing on a disease but there were so many other considerations.

"I've been tested since my last boyfriend and you don't have to worry about pregnancy. I can't have children." She was fussing with her bra and it was hard to focus on getting his own clothes on as he admired the curve of her back.

Wait, what? She'd said she couldn't have children as if she were telling him that she'd run out of milk. But this was life-changing news. He remembered her words in college: *I want three children. Two will fight with each other too much. You need a third to balance them out and be a peacemaker.*

She was still fumbling with her bra and he stood and clasped it for her. She didn't move away from him but tensed as his fingers brushed her skin.

What the hell? Just a few minutes ago, she couldn't get enough of him. He'd asked her a couple of times if she was sure she wanted to keep going and all she gave him in return was a lustful moan.

She tugged down her shirt, looked around and moved to her purse, which she'd set on one of the side tables. His instinct was to let her go but that's what he'd done last time. No matter what happened, he didn't want to go back to that place where she looked at him with cold, unfeeling eyes.

He put his hand on her purse. "I don't want things to go back to the way they were. Talk to me. Please."

She eyed his hand on her purse and for a second he thought she was about to smack it. Then he saw her shoulders slump.

"It's fine, Sameer. I know what just happened between us was…intense. It was pent-up emotion and desire and anger and…and whatever else." She looked away from him. "I am good. This is good. Now we can go back to a business relationship."

She tugged at her purse but he kept his hand firmly on it. "If you want us to keep things platonic, I'll respect that. But I can't stop being your friend. Why can't you have children?"

She refused to meet his eyes and a knot formed in his stomach. "After the accident, they discovered I had an ectopic pregnancy and they had to remove both of my tubes."

Her words were cold and clinical but the pain in

her eyes cut through him like a dull-edged knife. She'd gotten pregnant the night they made love.

"The standard pregnancy test was done the night I was admitted to the hospital. It was too soon for any indication of pregnancy. A month later when I started having symptoms the doctors thought the fevers and low blood pressure I was experiencing were a result of my injuries. By the time they re-tested me and discovered I was pregnant, it was too late and an infection had spread to my uterus that left it scarred."

Her voice broke at the last bit and he stepped closer and touched her arm. She turned slightly toward him and he didn't hesitate to pull her into his arms.

"This fashion label is the only baby for me."

He was about to point out that there were other ways to have a baby, including adoption, but Nisha gave him that look. That look where she narrowed her eyes and pressed her lips together. It was the *I'm done with this conversation* look.

She stepped out of his embrace and picked up her purse. "Nisha, please stay. Just for a little while. I don't like you leaving like this. I want us to talk about what happened."

She hesitated, then shook her head.

This time he didn't stop her from leaving. He'd screwed up. Again.

Nine

Nisha had spent the last week with a spring in her step. Sameer hadn't been lying about the hype surrounding her show. The sneak peeks of her digital lookbook were a wild success. Three different fashion influencers had touted her designs on social media. There were so many requests for invitations that Sameer had come up with the idea of using one of their smaller conference rooms as overflow seating and livestreaming the show. Nisha thought the idea was terrible. Who would want to come to a live show and watch it from another room? Turned out there were sixty-three such people, including members of the press.

She walked into the conference room of the

Mahal hotel that they were using as a dressing area, balancing three different dresses on hangers. The clothing adjustments were endless and she had a sewing box with pre-threaded needles for the last-minute things she'd have to hand sew once the models got there.

"Oh thank God, there's coffee." It was barely 7:00 a.m. and Jessica was already there working furiously on her laptop. The buffet table was scheduled to be filled later with food for the models, hair and makeup staff, technicians and the rest of the small army it took to put on a fashion show. Nisha hadn't thought to order breakfast for her and Jessica but was pleasantly surprised to see a small coffee and tea service setup along with pastries and fruit. Nisha had managed to make it out the door before her mother awoke so she hadn't had anything to eat.

"Sameer sent it."

Of course he did.

Frustratingly, the man was doing everything in his power to make her fall in love with him again. He had respected her boundaries over the last week. Even though they'd seen each other nearly every day, he kept things frustratingly distant and professional. It's what she wanted but not what she expected from him.

"You know he's been at it day and night working his family contacts to make sure you're getting buzz and using his own contacts to get buyers and stylists here. If it weren't for him, I don't know how we would've gotten it all done."

Nisha nodded as she mixed cream and sugar into her coffee and selected a muffin.

"You could be a little less cold to him, maybe show some appreciation for all he's done."

"We can make him a gift bag," she said half-jokingly.

Jessica rolled her eyes. Nisha took a seat next to her. "You know who I really need to thank? You! If it weren't for you, I wouldn't have a label, let alone a fashion show." She leaned over and hugged Jessica.

"He's not the guy you remember, Nisha."

He certainly isn't. Which was all the more reason to keep her distance. He was still the same sexy Sameer of her fantasies but not the self-absorbed, immature Sameer she hated. After that night a week ago when she'd climbed on top of him and had the most mind-blowing orgasm of her life, she'd done some serious soul searching.

The truth of it was that she had forgiven him. They'd both been immature. He'd never hidden his truth from her. She'd been there when he showed up to the college canteen hungover and unable to remember the name of the girl he'd slept with the night before. She'd put him in a taxi or driven him home when he'd had too much to drink. She had chosen to live a fantasy that one night with her would be so amazing that he'd magically change his ways and go from being a party boy to a settle-down-and-have-three-kids kind of man.

"He may have grown up some but it doesn't change the man that he is."

Jessica sighed. "Do you think maybe you're projecting all this anger that you've had after the accident onto him?" Nisha looked away. "The accident changed everything for you. You left your country, you couldn't be a model the way you wanted to. Plus all those surgeries. That has to be difficult for anyone. Have you considered that maybe Sameer has served as the punching bag for your anger?"

Nisha's stomach turned. What Jessica was saying made a lot of sense. She had been angry. Really angry. At her father for his infidelity, at her mother for putting up with it, at the accident, at herself for loving someone she couldn't have. She needed an outlet for her rage. Was Jessica right? Had she made Sameer the target because he was the easy villain?

"Let's focus on the show today. There are eight hours to go and a lot to do. I don't want to be thinking about Sameer."

"What's that about me?"

She whirled around to see him leaning against the door. He was dressed in jeans and a V-neck T-shirt. It was the kind of effortless sexy that Calvin Klein ads were made of. She herself was wearing leggings and a long-sleeve tunic, a light outfit to keep her cool while she ran around getting ready for the show. Yet, she suddenly felt hot. How long had he been standing there? How much had he heard?

"We were just talking about how grateful we are for all you've done," Jessica said smoothly. Nisha was glad because her tongue was stuck to the roof of her mouth and she couldn't stop staring at the little tuft of chest hair peeking out from the neck of his shirt. Had it just been a week since she'd rubbed her breasts against that chest, prickling with the feel of rough hair and hard muscle?

The corners of his mouth twitched and she suddenly realized that she'd been staring. The look on his face told her that he knew exactly what she'd been thinking about.

"I came to see if you needed anything." His eyes were locked on to hers.

You. I need you. Naked. And hard.

He raised a brow. "Anything. Just name it."

Her face grew hot and she looked away from him. "Thank you, I think we're good."

Jessica spoke up. "Actually, I was going over the final seating chart and I want to make sure that I have the right number of seats for your VIPs." She stood and handed him her tablet. While he looked down at the screen, she studied him. She'd always been attracted to him. Who wouldn't be? He was like a perfectly sliced piece of chocolate cake with layers of frosting. And unfortunately for her, she'd also had a taste of him and discovered that he was even better than her fantasies.

She took a large sip of her hot coffee just to get her mind on something else.

Jessica was standing next to Sameer and she made eyes at Nisha and tilted her head toward him. Nisha sighed. "Thank you for breakfast and everything else," Nisha managed.

"Wow, that almost sounded sincere." Sameer grinned to show her he was joking. She couldn't help but return his infectious smile and realized that he'd charmed her again. She just hoped that this time she'd survive his vortex.

Nisha's nerves were frayed as the show started. It was only going to be fifteen minutes long but every second would be packed. It didn't help that she was wearing a dress that hugged her body so tight that she was afraid she'd rip it if she bent the wrong way. As was tradition, she would walk out at the end of the show with the models and had to look fabulous wearing one of her own designs. A couple of weeks ago, the champagne-colored dress with black-and-silver embroidery seemed to be the perfect choice to complement the final red-and-silver showstopper. But, the short front hem and long train made it nearly impossible for Nisha to make last-minute adjustments on the models as they lined up to go onto the runway.

The professionals had done her hair and makeup and it seemed that a thousand pins were poking into her scalp. She knelt down on a knee to fix the lining of a skirt that had bunched up. The six-foot-tall model stood straight as Nisha quickly tacked a couple of stitches to make sure the lining stayed put. Her stomach was in a thousand knots. Despite the fittings and the preparations, there were so many things she was catching just minutes before the show. What had she missed?

Once she was done with the hem, she realized that her dress was so tight, she couldn't flex enough to get up from the position she was in. Cursing under her breath, she tried to remember the model's name and for the life of her couldn't do so. "Jessica!" she screamed, hoping it would catch the model's attention, but the woman stood frozen. She probably thought Nisha wanted a needle or a button.

"Need some help?"

Of course Sameer would come to her aid. He had some kind of uncanny sixth sense. He'd been doing this all day. She looked up and raised her arms in the universal give-me-a-hand-up gesture. He took her hands in his. They were strong and warm and sent sweet sensations through her body. He tugged, and as she stood, she tripped on the train of her dress and went stumbling into his arms. Her chest connected solidly with his and he let go of her hands and wrapped his arms around her. The dress was cut low in the back and his hands found her naked skin and sent shivers down her spine.

"You look amazing, by the way."

"Thanks," she mumbled, hoping he would let

her go. But he held on to her and she liked it. It was just the strength and warmth she needed to calm her nerves.

He bent his head and whispered in her ear. "You're going to do great. And I'll be in the front cheering you on."

His breath on her ear, the feel of his solid body, the way his thumb was moving across the naked parts of her back: it was all wreaking havoc on her senses. *Do we have enough time for you to take me to a private room and give me the release I need?*

He cleared his throat and dropped his arms. But not before she'd noticed him harden against her belly. He stepped away from her, his eyes black pools in the brightly lit room. "I'll see you after the show," he said hoarsely. Then he was gone and Jessica was at her side telling her they had three minutes and every seat was taken, including in the overflow room. The A-listers they'd been hoping for—social media influencers, magazine editors, buyers from the high-end department stores and celebrity stylists—were all in their seats drinking the *Nisha* cocktail and waiting to see Nisha's clothes.

Nisha took a breath. She walked down the line of models doing one final check.

Then the music started, the cue was called and off they went.

They had a total of forty items and thirty-five models. Late to the show calendar, they couldn't get enough models so the first five were their best ones and would do the final five looks as well. They had a total of nine minutes from the time they walked offstage to go back on. Jessica and a team of people waited with the change of clothes. The models had practiced the on and off.

There was applause from the audience as the first three models returned. They went to their assigned spots and were helped out of their clothes. One person took off jewelry and added new accessories and another put the clothes on. The models were professional and did not complain once as various people manhandled their breasts, stuffing them into the clothes so they appeared just right.

Nisha took a deep cleansing breath, bracing for her appearance. She barely heard the applause as the other models came back.

Jessica grabbed her arm. "You need to line up. The last two models will stay onstage, the MC will announce your name and you will walk to the end of the catwalk and stand. The models will come behind you and line the catwalk. When the song changes, you walk back in between the models and then pose again when you get to the start of the catwalk."

Nisha had practiced all this but appreciated the reminder because her nerves were so on edge, she couldn't remember a thing. She'd had to wear heels with the dress and crossed her fingers that she didn't trip and fall. She was no longer used to walking in heels, but thankfully the adrenaline running through her kept her from focusing on the pain in her leg.

She had modeled in college. The catwalk wasn't that foreign to her but she'd never been as nervous as she was now. Then the moment came. Her name was announced and she was walking onto the catwalk. They'd carefully chosen Bollywood music with a medium and even tempo. To save space, the catwalk was a simple floor-height, extralong design rather than the traditional T-shape. The seating was tiered and three rows deep along the catwalk, which went from the inside conference room right out to the outdoor tent. Rose had set up the tent beautifully with small white LED lights on the ceiling that looked like stars. It went with the night theme of the show.

As Nisha walked onto the catwalk, the audience burst into applause. Her legs were jelly and the shoes pinched her feet uncomfortably. She tried to breathe through the pain, knowing she was being stiff and not walking quite right. She saw her mother out of the corner of her eye but she had to focus on walking. *One foot in front of the other. Breathe. Breathe!* Her usual techniques weren't working and panic tightened her chest. Then she saw him. Sameer was in the front row at the end of the catwalk. He was standing, clapping and grinning so broadly that she couldn't help but smile back at him. The tension eased from her body and muscle memory kicked in. When she got to the end of the catwalk, she stopped and posed. The audience stood, clapping enthusiastically. Sameer blew her a kiss and without thinking, she blew one back. The music changed, her cue to walk back. When she turned, the models were lined up perfectly, spaced evenly along the catwalk, seventeen on each side. The showstopper was standing in the middle with a bouquet of flowers that she handed to Nisha. She turned to do one last pose for a final ovation.

The conference room ceilings were not high enough for them to do an ending fireworks explosion so Rose had come up with the idea of lighting up the ceiling and having thin silver tinsel fall on the catwalk.

It was perfect. The music, the lights, the show. Even if everyone hated her designs, this moment would keep her going.

When she returned backstage, she longed to take off her shoes but there was no time. The backstage room was packed with triple the number of people who had been there when she walked onto the stage. Rose and Jessica had ushered some of the A-listers into the room to get a closer peek at the clothes and meet Nisha. She lost track of all the hands she shook and promises she made. Jessica followed her with her trusty iPad and Nisha was once again thankful for her friend. She had no doubt Jessica would keep track of all these informal conversations and follow up.

It all went by quickly. There were three additional fashion shows on the official calendar after hers so few people lingered. Most of the models were working at least one other show so the backstage room soon cleared out. Rose came through to issue instructions to the hotel staff to clean up the room. Sameer was chatting with Jessica. It looked like a hurricane had gone through the space. There was litter covering the floor. Thread, needles, buttons, makeup brushes, cotton balls, pieces of random fabric, hangers—they were scattered everywhere. Nisha made a note to tip the cleaning crew really well.

She plopped into a chair, took off her shoes and slipped on her flats. Her leg hurt like hell.

"Nisha, you need to rest." Her mom had been waiting patiently and now came and gave her a hug.

"Ma, can you believe it? All that we've been through the last few years was for this night."

"I am so proud of you." Her mother kissed her forehead. "But I'm worried about you. I saw those heels you were wearing. I am going to go ask Sameer to get you to a hotel room."

"Ma, no!" Really? Her mother was going to ask the fox to take her little hen to a hotel room? But her mother was already screaming Sameer's name and he dutifully walked over.

"*Beta*, is there a place where Nisha can rest? All this standing on her feet is not good for her leg."

Sameer frowned. "What's wrong with her leg?" Her mother launched into an explanation of how her knees and femur had been crushed in the accident and she'd needed multiple surgeries and physical therapy to recover but her leg had never been a hundred percent. The look of horror that crossed Sameer's face tugged at her heart.

"Auntie, I'll take care of her. Don't worry. You go home and I'll make sure that she keeps her foot up for the rest of the day."

"Thank you, *beta*."

"Wait, do I get a say in this?"

Her mother shook her head. "Look at your ankle, it is already swelling. You need to go to a room right now and put your feet up."

Sameer placed an arm around her mom and led her to the door, assuring her that he would take good care of Nisha. The sight of her mother being so familiar with Sameer should have bothered her but it didn't anymore. There was a time when her mother used to literally pinch his cheeks and spoil him with gifts. Her mother's relationship with Sameer predated hers. Once again she was reminded of just how much her mother had given up for her.

After putting her mother in a hotel car, Sameer returned. "All right, Cinderella, the glass slippers are off, it's time to take you to your carriage."

Ten

"If you bring out a wheelchair, I will throw my heels at you."

Sameer smiled. If he could have his way, he would pick her up in his arms and take her straight to his bedroom but he didn't dare suggest it.

"Why don't you lean on me so you don't have to put a lot of weight on your foot." He offered her his hand and she gave it to him. Once she was standing, he put his arm around her waist. "Put your weight on me." He kept focused on the task of taking her to the penthouse rather than acknowledge how good it felt to have her in his arms. How right she felt against him.

"Where are we going?"

"To the penthouse."

He tried not to think about the fact that it was where they'd had hot, lusty sex just a week ago. He'd been living there and had been unable to look at the sofa without feeling her soft skin against his, without remembering how right she'd felt against him, how well they had moved together and how much he wanted her.

"You have two hundred–some rooms. Can't I use one of those?"

"The hotel is fully booked because of Fashion Week. Don't worry, the penthouse has five bedrooms. We can find you one that is the farthest away from mine. I promise to leave you alone."

It was a promise he wasn't sure he could keep. It had been pure torture keeping things business-like with her over the past week. It was clear that whatever happened between them last week had nothing to do with the present and everything to do with the past. He had to establish a new relationship with her, on her terms.

She leaned into his solid body, and the memory of her kissing him, touching him, making him go mad with desire, flooded his mind. They rode the elevator in silence. He took her directly to the second floor of the penthouse, where the bedrooms were located. He helped her into a room that was simply decorated with a platform bed, white comforter and a black dresser.

He fluffed pillows behind her and placed one

under the knee of her right leg. She was putting on a brave face but he could tell that she was in pain. The adrenaline of the show had worn off and she was finally feeling the strain she'd put her body under. He was the one responsible for her physical condition. Compared with her, he'd gotten off without a scratch.

She was removing pins from her hair and winced as she tugged too hard.

"You need some help?"

She gave him a long look, then sighed. "Yes, the glam squad did my hair and they put like a thousand pins in it. I don't even know where they all are."

He went to the other side of the bed and climbed on. She tensed. "Turn a little bit so I can see your head."

She turned away from him and he knelt beside her, the soft bed making it hard for him to keep his balance. There really were a million pins in her hair. He started with the easiest-looking ones. She held out her hand and he put the assortment of pins in her palm. One by one the strands of her hair loosened and fell onto her shoulders.

He was barely touching her but he could sense the tension and heat coming off her body. He wasn't the only one who was insanely turned on right now. But he wouldn't be the one to act on it. While he had no doubt that if he leaned down and kissed the back of her neck, she would melt right into his arms, he wasn't going to do it.

Once all the pins were out and her hair cascaded down her shoulders, he moved down the bed without looking at her.

He gently took her foot.

"What are you doing?"

"I am rubbing your foot. And if you let me, I can massage your leg. Your ma mentioned that massage helps with the pain."

She reached over into her purse, which she'd put on the side table, and got out a tub of cream. "Do you mind rubbing this on my leg?" He read the label on the tube.

"Ayurvedic cream?"

She nodded. He squeezed some onto his hands and then began rubbing it on her foot, working his way up her calf. Her skin was smooth and silky and he kept his eyes focused on her feet. She was still wearing the dress she'd worn onto the catwalk. The skintight, slightly see-through fabric left little to the imagination, not that he needed to imagine much. He just needed to close his eyes to experience what it would feel like to run his hand up her thigh all the way to her core, to know what it felt like to be inside her.

He shifted on the bed to hide the effect that touching her was having on him. "Does the ayurvedic stuff work?"

"Better than you'd think. With all of the surgeries and physical therapy, I didn't want to get hooked

FREE BOOKS GIVEAWAY

2 FREE
SIZZLING
ROMANCE
BOOKS!

2 FREE
PASSIONATE
ROMANCE
BOOKS!

GET UP TO FOUR FREE BOOKS & TWO FREE GIFTS WORTH OVER $20!

We pay for everything!

See Details Inside

YOU pick your books –
WE pay for everything.
You get up to FOUR New Books and
TWO Mystery Gifts...absolutely FREE

Dear Reader,

I am writing to announce the launch of a huge **FREE BOOKS GIVEAWAY**... and to let you know that YOU are entitled to choose up to FOUR fantastic books that WE pay for.

Try **Harlequin® Desire** books featuring the worlds of the American elite with juicy plot twists, delicious sensuality and intriguing scandal.

Try **Harlequin Presents® Larger-Print** books featuring the glamourous lives of royals and billionaires in a world of exotic locations, where passion knows no bounds.

Or TRY BOTH!

In return, we ask just one favor: Would you please participate in our brief Reader Survey? We'd love to hear from you.

This FREE BOOKS GIVEAWAY means that your introductory shipment is completely free, <u>even the shipping</u>! If you decide to continue, you can look forward to curated monthly shipments of brand-new books from your selected series, always at a discount off the cover price! <u>Plus you can cancel any time</u>. Who could pass up a deal like that?

Sincerely

Pam Powers

Pam Powers
For Harlequin Reader Service

Complete the survey below and return it today to receive up to **4 FREE BOOKS** and **FREE GIFTS** guaranteed!

FREE BOOKS GIVEAWAY
Reader Survey

1

Do you prefer stories with happy endings?

◯ YES ◯ NO

2

Do you share your favorite books with friends?

◯ YES ◯ NO

3

Do you often choose to read instead of watching TV?

◯ YES ◯ NO

YES! Please send me my Free Rewards, consisting of **2 Free Books from each series I select** and **Free Mystery Gifts**. I understand that I am under no obligation to buy anything, no purchase necessary see terms and conditions for details.

❏ Harlequin Desire® (225/326 HDL GRQJ)
❏ Harlequin Presents® Larger-Print (176/376 HDL GRQJ)
❏ Try Both (225/326 & 176/376 HDL GRQU)

FIRST NAME	LAST NAME

ADDRESS

APT.#	CITY

STATE/PROV.	ZIP/POSTAL CODE

EMAIL ❏ Please check this box if you would like to receive newsletters and promotional emails from Harlequin Enterprises ULC and its affiliates. You can unsubscribe anytime.

HD/HP-122-FBG22

BUSINESS REPLY MAIL
FIRST-CLASS MAIL   PERMIT NO. 717   BUFFALO, NY

POSTAGE WILL BE PAID BY ADDRESSEE

HARLEQUIN READER SERVICE
PO BOX 1341
BUFFALO NY 14240-8571

NO POSTAGE
NECESSARY
IF MAILED
IN THE
UNITED STATES

▲ If offer card is missing write to: Harlequin Reader Service, P.O. Box 1341, Buffalo, NY 14240-8531 or visit www.ReaderService.com ▲

on pain pills." She put a hand to her mouth. "I'm so sorry, Sameer, I wasn't thinking."

He gave her a small smile but he couldn't meet her eyes. "You always were smarter and stronger than me. I didn't think about the fact that taking them for so long would get me hooked until it was too late."

"Are you still in pain?"

He stared steadfastly at her foot. The silence stretched between them. How did he tell her that after the accident, he had only focused on himself. When he heard that Nisha and her mom had moved to America, he used that as an excuse to assume that she was okay. If he was honest with himself, he'd been ashamed to face her again. It was only after he'd gotten sober that he realized that she was on the top of the list of people he needed to make amends to. Despite what Nisha said, he still blamed himself for the accident, but he was slowly realizing that his crime was a lot worse than breaking her body—it was breaking her heart.

After what seemed like forever, he finally looked up. "It wasn't nearly as bad for me as it was for you. I healed completely. I don't have lasting effects. I was just weak."

She leaned forward and put a hand on his arm. "I can't take the credit. It was my mom. She was the one who began teaching me yoga for pain relief and looking into homeopathic and ayurvedic medicines. If it weren't for her, I don't know how I would've managed."

He was sure his family would have done the same for him. If he'd let them. But he had pushed them away, too ashamed and afraid to let them see his weaknesses. Instead he had looked for artificial ways to clear the pain in his heart.

"I'm sorry, Nisha. You don't know how many times I wish I'd put you in a taxi that night. You are still suffering and I've been totally fine." Perhaps it was his karmic justice to live with the guilt for the rest of his life.

"The accident wasn't your fault. Even if you'd put me in a taxi, that car would still have been on the road and veered into the wrong lane. Who knows, it could have been worse." She scooted closer to him. "Ma told me what you went through. You were in the hospital for the better part of a year, and then the addiction and rehab. None of it was easy for either one of us."

His heart clenched. She was the one literally in pain and yet here she was making him feel better. "You know the one thing I regret more than anything, it's the way I treated you. Not just after the accident but also before."

She pulled away from his touch and sat cross-legged on the bed.

It had hit him when he was walking her mother out from the show. *Sameer, beta, I don't understand why there is so much tension between you and Nisha. She has always loved you, even when she was a child. Nisha thinks I don't know but a mother sees everything. The accident didn't hurt her as much as the separation from you. The morning of the accident, she came to me and asked me to take her* rishta *to your mother.*

On the day he had broken up with her, she had asked her mother to go talk to his family about them getting married. He knew they were close but how had he missed the fact that she was that serious about him? Whenever they'd talked about their future goals, she'd always been obsessed with becoming a top model and had even talked about entering the Miss World contest. Marriage had never been in her vocabulary. Or maybe he just hadn't paid close enough attention.

He swallowed. "I didn't realize what that night really meant to you, and for that I'm sorry. Sleeping with you was the best thing I ever did and the worst mistake I ever made."

She inhaled sharply so he continued quickly. "Don't get me wrong, you were the only person in my life who was in my corner, no matter how much of a shit I was. With everyone else, I was nothing but a party boy. Especially compared to Arjun. You were the only person in my life who looked at me without judgment. The only reason I regretted that night is because I was scared of losing you from my life."

"So you did the one thing that you knew would hurt me?"

"I thought I was making sure that I didn't make things worse. You know how I was with women back then. I knew if we kept having sex, I'd screw it up and then I'd lose you from my life."

He reached out and took her hand. She didn't resist. He locked eyes with her. "I loved you. I loved you the way I've never loved anyone in my life. After we had sex, I was so scared of losing you that I needed us to go back to the way things were, because if we started dating, I would screw up. I would drink and cheat on you and there was no coming back from that. Then after the accident, I knew that I had to take myself out of your life so I didn't wreck it any more than I already had."

Her eyes were shining and she squeezed his hand. "You not being in my life is what wrecked me."

His chest constricted so painfully that he was sure his heart was literally breaking. Despite everything he'd done, she still cared about him. It was written all over her face.

He lifted her hand to his face and kissed it. "What we did a week ago really messed me up."

She tilted her head and he swallowed against his tight throat. *You have a tendency to bottle up how you're really feeling and then you externalize your inner angst through self-destructive behavior.* The advice he'd gotten from his therapist in rehab had been playing in his mind for the last week. Every time he'd seen Nisha, the words were on his lips—to tell her how he really felt. But he'd held back. Now the show was over, it had been a success, and if he didn't tell her now, it might be too late.

"I care for you, Nisha. I've missed having you in my life. I thought after the accident it would be better to be without you." He swallowed. "When I saw you again, I realized that you were the piece that's been missing, the piece that has kept me from healing completely."

Her eyes were full of tears now and he cupped her face, wiping a tear away with his thumb. She leaned into his hand and his chest constricted even more.

"I know last week was about your anger but it made me realize just how much I've lost."

She opened her mouth to say something but he put a finger to her lips. He needed to say it all. "But I don't deserve you, nor should I ever have you. I know if we get together, I'll screw it up. I'll do something boneheaded that'll hurt you and I'm not willing to take that chance."

She closed her eyes and a few tears squeezed out of them, dripping down her cheeks. Those tears burned his heart like little drops of lava. Then she shook her head. "I'm not going to let you do this to me again." She opened her eyes and despite the fact that they were filled with tears, the anger in them was clear.

She sat up, scooted toward him and grabbed a fistful of his shirt. Their noses touched and he wanted to lean in and kiss her. To lay her back on the bed and touch and lick every inch of her, to make love to her the way he'd always wanted to and never had the chance to. He needed to show her just how much she meant to him. But he wouldn't. It was time for him to grow the hell up and do the right thing. He needed to think about her, not himself.

"I have loved you all my life. There was a time when you were my entire world."

His breath hitched. Loved. Past tense. He'd had something beautiful and he'd ruined it. It's what he always did. When he was in college, he had a motorcycle that he'd lovingly kept in pristine condition. He'd personally cleaned the filter, adjusted the chain and kept up the fluid levels on a daily basis. On a hard ride, he'd taken a curve too fast. He had walked away with some scratches but the bike hadn't fared as well. He'd taken it to the best shop but the bike was never the same. No matter how many hours he spent cleaning and oiling every part, the engine never purred the same way. *It'll never be the same with Nisha. I've caused too much damage.*

"Since I can remember, you've dictated the terms of our relationship. Not anymore." She leaned forward, her nose nearly touching his. "You aren't backing away now. We are doing this. We are going to be together."

He moved back so he could look her in the eyes. *What is she saying?*

"Nisha, I don't trust myself with you. I don't want to hurt you ever again."

"I'm a grown woman, not the clueless girl you

used to know. I can take care of myself. My life has been in limbo for eight years playing endless versions of what-if scenarios between us. I need to know whether we sink or swim together. It's time for you to give me something right here, right now."

"I'll give you anything you want." His throat was tight. How could she want to be with him after everything he'd done? What he deserved was what she'd initially given him, anger, hatred, admonition.

"Then I want you to help me run my fashion label. I want you to make your every waking moment about me…" She poked him in the chest with a finger. "Most importantly, I want you to be my love slave, at my beck and call."

He smiled. As well as he thought he knew her, she always had a way of surprising him. She leaned in and flicked her tongue against his lips, then pressed her mouth to his. He returned her salty kiss with an urgent fervor. As he deepened the kiss, she reached between his legs. He was already hard but he wanted this time to be different. He didn't want it to be about comfort or anger or even lust. He needed this to be about showing her that he cared, that he was done being a selfish ass. He grabbed her hand.

"Where is the zipper on this dress?"

She smiled. "It doesn't have one. It was stitched on, you have to take the seam apart." She showed him the side seam, which already had some tears in it.

"Are you telling me that I can literally rip this off you?"

That got him a giggle. A legit, girlie giggle that he hadn't heard from her since before that fateful night. A giggle that used to warm his heart, and one that he was afraid was gone forever. He smiled and kissed the part of her waist that peeked through the tear in the dress.

"Let me show you how to take out the stitches. This fabric is really expensive and I'd like to be able to fix the dress."

"You're thinking about the cost of fabric right now?"

"Don't you remember that it was my cash-strapped business that brought you back into my life?"

She was starting to carefully break through the stitches in the ripped seam. He bent his head and kissed her fingers as her hands worked the stitches. She wasn't the girl he had known. The Nisha before him was a confident, mature woman who knew how to get what she wanted. And she wanted him.

Once the dress was opened to her breasts, she rolled it down her body and peeled pads off her nipples. She hadn't been wearing a bra. The gesture was so mundane yet sexy that he lost track of what he was doing. He cupped one breast and kissed the other, gently sucking on her hardened nipple. She moaned and he gently pushed her back onto the bed. He slid the dress down her hips and nearly lost his mind when he saw the tiny lace thong she was wearing. He couldn't even wait long enough to take it off. He needed to taste her now.

He pushed the thong aside and licked her core. She arched her back and moaned so he sucked and licked some more and put his finger inside her. She was wet and tight and his own body screamed in response but he ignored his desire. Today was about her. He increased the tempo of his finger, matching the rhythm of her hips. It didn't take long for her to scream in pleasure and buck her hips. He felt a ripple of heat run through him to see her like this. How had he gotten through the last eight years without her?

She was satiated but he didn't want to stop. For once he didn't care about his own pleasure, a first with him. He wasn't a selfish lover but he usually cared about himself just as much as his partner. But not now. Even as she lifted herself off the bed, he gently pushed her back down. "I'm not done with you."

"Sameer." The breathless way she said his name was all the encouragement he needed. He took her thong off and put his mouth back on her core, enjoying the smell and taste of her. It took a little longer the second time but it was clear she enjoyed it just as much. When he was done, he positioned himself next to her feet. She tried to sit up but he stopped her. It wasn't that he didn't want her. She looked exhausted and he remembered that the reason she was in this room was to rest her leg. He grabbed her foot and began rubbing it.

"Sameer, that's not fair."

He smiled at her. "Didn't you tell me that I owe you a few dozen favors?"

"If you think that counted as one, you're mistaken."

"Good, then I owe you a few dozen more of those too."

"That foot rub is going to put me to sleep."

He leaned over and kissed her lightly on the lips. "I would love nothing more than for you to be so relaxed around me that you can sleep."

He tucked her under the sheets, then lifted one end so he could continue rubbing her feet and legs. It didn't take long for her to close her eyes. He watched her for a while, his thoughts racing a mile a minute. So much had happened in such a short period of time, he hadn't fully processed it. Nor did he want to. It all felt right in the here and now and he was going to enjoy the moment of content.

He texted her mother to let her know that Nisha had fallen asleep and would not be home. He left out the part that she was in his penthouse. Appearances were important. He wasn't sure how conservative her mother was, nor did he really know how Reeta Auntie would feel about them being together.

He tucked a pillow under Nisha's leg, then climbed under the comforter. He was a night owl, and it was too early for bed, but he wanted to be near her, take in the heat of her body next to his, let her perfume permeate his soul. She was naked but he left his clothes on. He knew the temptation would be too much for him to resist and she definitely needed some rest.

He clicked through his messages and almost woke Nisha. Her show was a hit. There were several social media posts showcasing her dresses and lots of press buzz around the exciting new designer. Vinod had sent him a message that one of the high-end department stores had contacted him for a price quote on five of her runway designs and wanted a deal for an exclusive line of clothes. While the details had yet to be worked out, that deal alone would make Nisha's business solvent. Even Arjun texted to congratulate him.

A wave of relief washed over him. He hadn't realized how much he needed her label to succeed. No matter what Nisha said, he needed to make amends to her, and making her business successful let him absolve himself of the guilt he still felt. Now that the show was over, they could focus on their relationship, find a way back from the pain and mistrust between them.

His phone buzzed with another email from Vinod and when he read the text, his body went cold.

Eleven

When Nisha woke, she was thoroughly confused. She was in a strange, dark room, naked under the bedsheets and feeling a new sense of happiness. Her phone was on the bedside table. She clicked it on to see it was 3:00 a.m. Then it all came back. The show, the conversation with Sameer, and him giving her not one but two mind-blowing orgasms. Had that all just happened a few hours ago? Then she sat up straighter. Her mother would be worried sick about her. She didn't stay overnight with anyone, not even when she was dating. If nothing else, she always kept up appearances with her traditional mother. It was a matter of respect.

She swung her legs off the bed and discovered her

ruined dress and panties on the floor. She groaned. Though she had a change of clothes, she'd left the bag in the conference room downstairs. There was a robe in the closet, which she belted tightly. She used the attached bathroom to wash her face. The fabulous makeup from the show was smeared all over her face, making her look like the bride of Frankenstein. It took all of the little hotel soaps and washcloths to scrub the makeup from her face.

Is this real? Two months ago, Sameer seemed like a dream. Now she was living her adolescent fantasies.

She made her way downstairs. There was a light on in the kitchen. Sameer was sitting at the kitchen island, clicking away on a laptop. He was wearing sweatpants and a T-shirt, her favorite outfit on him. His hair was mussed and her body reacted instantly. She was within touching distance when he noticed her.

"You're up."

"You should have woken me up. Ma will be worried. I need to change my clothes and get home…"

"I already texted your mom." He stood and pulled her into his arms. His body was warm and strong and she nestled into it.

"Since when did you become the responsible one?"

"There's a lot about me that's changed."

She rested her head on his chest. From what she'd seen so far, he had truly become the man of her dreams. But there was still a thorn in her chest that had her questioning if she could trust him with her heart again.

He nuzzled her neck and she felt his erection pressing against her belly. "Have I told you how beautiful you are?" Heat coursed through her body and she rubbed herself sensually against him. While she'd enjoyed him going down on her, she wanted him inside her.

He groaned. "You know, I haven't been able to look at that sofa since last week."

She grinned, took his hand and led him to the couch. She pushed him down onto it, removed her robe as he shed his sweatpants. She straddled him. This time their lovemaking was slower, sweeter, and at the end, she felt something quite different from what she had before. She was fulfilled, happy, content— emotions she hadn't felt for a very long time.

Even after they were done, she sat straddling him. He pushed her hair out of the way and cupped her face, gazing at her. Then he ran his thumbs over her forehead, where her scar was, and he frowned. "Is this from the accident?"

She nodded, surprised he'd noticed. Even without makeup, the scar was barely visible and they were sitting in a semi-dark room.

He kissed the scar. "One more thing that I have to make up for."

She moved his hands from her face and squeezed them tightly. "If we're going to make this work, you have to let go of the accident. You can't blame your-self every time my leg hurts or you see the scar. I don't want you to treat me like your penance."

He shook his head vehemently. "That's not at all how I think of you. I see you as a woman I was too stupid to appreciate."

"Then appreciate me now. Appreciate and antici-pate our future. Don't live in the past."

He nodded and she knew it was something they'd have to work on together. She slid off him. "By any chance did anyone find my bag of clothes in the conference room downstairs?"

He nodded and pointed to her bag on the couch. "Jessica dropped it off."

She slid off him. "I don't know what I'd do with-out her."

"Actually, I need to talk to you about Jessica."

The look on Nisha's face told him that this would not be an easy conversation to have and it wasn't one he wanted to. He'd spent the last five hours poring over the financial spreadsheets that Vinod had sent him. He and Nisha had just gotten to a good place; they were at the start of what he hoped would be a healing relationship. He didn't want to give her bad news but he had no choice. Vinod had already alerted Jessica and he wanted Nisha to hear it di-rectly from him.

"There's no easy way to tell you so I'm just going to say it." He swallowed and noticed that Nisha had taken a step back from him and was belting her robe.

"Jessica has been embezzling money from you."

Nisha's eyes widened. "That's not possible. Jessica would never do anything like that."

He motioned for her to come to his laptop. He knew that he couldn't make accusations without showing her the proof. He brought up the first screen, which was her bank statement. "Here are the payments she made from your company account to the fabric vendors."

"I know it's a lot more than our projections but remember that prices went up because of global supply chain issues. Plus, we needed expedited shipping."

He nodded. "That's what we thought at first. But Vinod is meticulous about this stuff. He got the original receipt from the fabric vendor." He clicked on a PDF document.

"He has been asking Jessica for the receipts but she keeps putting him off. He got frustrated and called the vendor directly for a copy. The vendor told him that they were revising the receipt as Jessica requested, which made him suspicious."

"There could be a million reasons why she requested a revised invoice. We made a deal with the vendor to pay within fifteen days of receiving the invoice in exchange for them expediting the order shipment. She probably paid them as soon as the invoice came in and figured she would sort out any issues after the show."

He knew this wouldn't be easy. He couldn't accuse Jessica without conclusive proof. Nisha was and always had been fiercely loyal to her friends.

He pointed to the invoice. "Does anything jump out at you?"

Nisha stared at the screen. "I'm very attentive to the fabrics I select because there is such variation in costs. A bolt could be three dollars a yard or thirty thousand dollars a yard. I try to keep my selections mid-range. I don't remember the exact cost of each bolt but this looks about right. I know the ones I selected for the show are a little more expensive but…" She stopped and he exhaled. "What's this twenty percent charge for agent commission?" she asked.

"That's what Vinod caught. When he asked the vendor, they said it was a fee that they paid to Jessica for bringing your business to them."

Nisha stepped back. "There has to be some mistake."

"That was my first thought. I had Vinod track down original receipts for the other big purchases. Your vendors in India haven't sent everything, but he talked to the people you used for the swag bag materials and they said that they paid a ten percent fee back to a US bank account for the agent. They specifically said that Jessica gave them the bank account number."

He wished he didn't have to tell Nisha the news

because the look on her face seared through his heart.

"I'll talk to Jessica. She gave up a high-paying Wall Street job to come work with me at a fraction of her salary. She's spent day and night to make this successful. There is no way she's embezzling."

"I sincerely hope that's the case. But until we investigate it, Jessica can't work for you."

Nisha shook her head. "No. This is my company and I'll deal with it. You can't do anything until I've talked to Jessica."

Sameer swallowed. He'd asked Vinod to wait but Vinod reported to Arjun and not to him. Arjun had asked Vinod to fire Jessica immediately.

Nisha gave him a hard look, then picked up her phone. Sameer had set it to do not disturb mode to make sure she got some rest.

"I have a lot of messages from Jessica here. You already called her, didn't you?" Nisha's face was red. She whirled, picked up her bag of clothes and marched upstairs. He followed her but she literally shut the door to the bedroom in his face. He waited outside. She emerged a few minutes later dressed in jeans and a T-shirt and gave him a hard look.

"Jessica left me five voice mails and more than twenty text messages telling me that she has an explanation that Vinod wouldn't listen to. He used some clause in the contract to tell her that if she accessed the *Nisha* business accounts, he would take legal action against her. That woman gave up her life to make my label a success."

"Nisha, it's not the way I would've done things. Can we talk about how to handle this situation?"

"Sameer, Arjun may have been pulling the strings but this is totally your style. You just throw people away."

She might as well have fired a bullet straight into his heart. Earlier in the evening he'd thought they'd finally had an understanding and gone back to a place of love and trust. That whatever happened, they had learned to communicate with each other. But that wasn't the case at all.

Sameer insisted on getting one of the hotel town cars to take her home. Nisha directed the driver to her studio. She didn't want to face her mother. The studio was her happy place, the place where she forgot everything and sketched her designs, then brought them to life with fabric and thread.

The street was eerily quiet when she disembarked from the car. The city that never sleeps apparently slept in the wee hours of the morning. Many of the businesses, including hers, had the grates open on the sidewalk. It was where trash was stored until the morning pickup. She wrinkled her nose as she made her way toward the studio and cursed when she nearly stepped into the damned pothole. The town car driver rolled down the window to ask if she was okay and she nodded.

She used her finger to open the studio doors. The locks were biometric. She moved to put her code into the alarm system but it was already disengaged. She frowned. All of the staff who had direct access to the studio were schooled in making sure they turned the alarm on when they left. It wasn't just about preventing thugs from stealing stuff from the studio. Industrial espionage was as bad in the fashion industry as anywhere else. There were any number of designers whose styles had been stolen from their studios. Jessica even had an app that informed her when that alarm wasn't activated so she could turn it on remotely.

Then she realized that Jessica had been summarily fired by a bunch of strangers and tears stung her eyes. She didn't know what hurt more, that Jessica had possibly betrayed her, or the fact that Sameer hadn't considered what firing her best friend would do to her. The Sameer she had thought had changed still did what was best for him without considering how it affected others.

She closed the door behind her, took out her cell phone and punched 911 without hitting the call button. "Hello!" she cried out into the open space.

Jessica emerged from her office and Nisha breathed out in relief. She canceled the call on her phone.

"I'm so glad you're here." Nisha walked toward Jessica and noticed that her eyes were red and puffy.

"I just came to clean out my personal stuff from

the office. I didn't want to be here when everyone arrived."

Nisha put her arms around her and hugged her tightly. "I fell asleep and didn't get any of your messages. I'm so sorry! I don't believe any of it."

She led Jessica to the kitchenette and used the single-cup brewer to make each of them a cup of coffee. Jessica wrapped her hands around the hot mug. Nisha waited.

"I didn't want to stress you out right before the show. You had so much to do with getting the new clothes ready. I was behind on my rent and my landlord had given me notice. He would've evicted me a week ago. I didn't know what to do. I knew that the show would be a success and you'd back-pay me. I just had to hold out that long. So, I added an extra charge to our fabric purchases and asked the vendor to wire that money separately to me. I figured once we were finally solvent, I would pay it back."

Nisha's stomach clenched. She hadn't believed that Jessica had actually taken the money but it was right in her face. Jessica looked miserable and Nisha realized that her friend was risking a lot by admitting the fraud to her. "Why didn't you tell me?"

"You were already so stressed between the show and Sameer coming back, I didn't want to dump more on you. And I didn't think that it would even get noticed, in the grand scheme of things. It was only a few thousand dollars."

"Then what about the other kickbacks?"

Jessica hung her head. "It was so easy the first time, I thought I would do it for a few more invoices to have a cash reserve in case things didn't go well. The first one paid my back rent but if we didn't get orders soon enough after the show, then I'd be in the same situation. I can't afford to lose my apartment. It's rent stabilized. If I lose it, I can't afford the current New York rent prices on this salary." Tears were now streaming down her face. Guilt coursed through Nisha. She hadn't been able to pay Jessica the salary she had promised.

"I don't have a safety net. My savings covered rent for a while. My parents live in a trailer in Ohio. They have even less money than I do. If I lost my apartment, I'd have nowhere to go."

Nisha stood and hugged her friend. "You always have me, Jessica. I would've taken care of you. You know you can come live with me if something like that happened. For God's sake, I spent weeks on your couch."

"I swear I was going to pay the money back to the business. It was just safety until we had cash flowing in again. I know how you feel about asking your father for money and I just…" She put her head in her hands.

Nisha's stomach churned. She'd been so selfish. Jessica had supported her every step of the way and she'd been so focused on battling with—and now sleeping with—Sameer that she hadn't noticed her friend's pain.

Jessica stood and went to the office. When she returned, she had her laptop and a piece of paper. "Here are the bank statements from the account where the cash went. Look…" Jessica pointed and Nisha saw that the bank account had been established in both Jessica's name and the company's. There were several deposits totaling nearly a hundred thousand dollars but there had only been one withdrawal for nine thousand dollars three weeks ago. "I only took out what I needed to pay the landlord."

Nisha rubbed her neck. Jessica could and should have come to Nisha earlier. She'd betrayed her trust. But Nisha couldn't bear the thought of losing her. How would she manage the business on her own?

Jessica gave her a piece of paper stating she owed the business nine thousand dollars, which she requested six months to pay back.

Nisha didn't have to think about it. She tore the letter into shreds. Jessica had put the bank account in the company name and hadn't pocketed all the money. Her intentions weren't bad. "What we need to do is get out of the contract with the Mahal hotels. I wouldn't have gotten this far without you and I'm not going to let them push you out."

Jessica stared at her. "You can't do that. Not for me."

Nisha shook her head. "You should have talked to me. No matter what we're going through, you're my friend and I would've figured out a way to help you. But you made a mistake, one I believe you'll never make again."

Jessica hugged her. "I'm so, so sorry."

"Okay, how do we get rid of the Mahal hotels?"

Jessica sighed. "It's not going to be easy. They own fifty percent of the company until their investment plus interest is paid back on schedule. Our contract terms are generous but if we want to dissolve the partnership earlier than three years, we have to pay them back right away plus double interest."

"How soon can we make a deal on the advance orders?"

Jessica shrugged. "While there's a lot of buzz, people are busy with Fashion Week and it could be a month or more before we start getting anywhere."

Nisha and Jessica pored over the company's finances and ran some numbers based on the preliminary interest they'd gotten from buyers. The only real order had come in from a stylist for the dress Nisha had worn on the catwalk for her celebrity client. That dress would bring in fifteen thousand dollars and Nisha cursed herself for having let Sameer get rough with the fabric. The cost of the fabric alone was nearly one thousand dollars. Then she thought about what he'd done after he'd taken the dress off her and some of her anger dissipated.

They could pay back the money that Jessica had taken out but it was barely a dent in what they owed the Mahal Group. Nisha needed some big department store orders to make that happen. Plus, there was the money she owed her father for the initial investment. At the moment, she didn't know whom she wanted out of her life more, the Mahal Group, or her father. She couldn't even think about what she wanted with Sameer.

"There's no choice, Nisha. I have to leave the company. Vinod made it very clear there was no other option. I'll reprint that letter. Maybe my old boss on Wall Street will take me back."

"You're not paying back the money. In fact, I'm pretty sure we signed an employment contract for you and I've only been paying you a small part of what you're supposed to be making. If we're stuck with the Mahal Group, they better well back-pay you."

"While I appreciate the sentiment, you shouldn't do that, Nisha. It'll make your working relationship with Sameer tougher."

Our relationship is complicated enough. What's one more issue?

She smiled at her friend. "It's the least I can do for you."

Which is more than she could say for Sameer. With each minute that passed, Nisha was even more upset at him. When things got tough, he took the easy way out. He hadn't even had the courtesy to call Jessica and talk to her himself. He'd let Vinod do the hard part.

"Try not to blame Sameer."

Nisha shook her head. "This might not have been his decision but he didn't do anything to stop it either. He hasn't changed a bit."

* * *

Nisha entered her apartment after an eighteen-hour day at the studio. With Jessica leaving, all of the minutiae—details of payroll, vendor payments and follow-ups from the show—had fallen to Nisha. It hadn't taken her long to miss her friend. Jessica had done everything she could to leave things organized for Nisha, which made her all the more angry at Sameer.

A week had gone by since she'd last seen him. He'd called every day but she'd put him off. She was too angry to deal with him. In the last year, Jessica was the person who had kept her going, who had assured her that despite the many setbacks Nisha would be successful. And now that *Nisha* was a success, Jessica wouldn't be there to celebrate with her. It was all wrong.

Her mother was not only waiting for her but had made her favorite comfort food. An *aloo paratha*, a layered bread stuffed with potatoes, and *dahi*, a homemade yogurt. She realized that she'd drunk coffee all day and nibbled on a couple of power bars. Her stomach was complaining and she sat down at the kitchen counter and gratefully wolfed down the first *paratha*. Her mother put the *tava* on the stove and warmed up another.

"Your show was such a success, why do you have so much tension?"

Nisha didn't feel like rehashing what had happened with Jessica. Nor could she ever share what was really weighing on her: the fact that she missed Sameer. At least the last time it was just one night together. Now his body was imprinted on hers. The smell of his cologne, the feel of his breath against her skin, the memory of his tongue against her core would haunt her for the rest of her life. She didn't know what the future held for them but in the present, she wasn't prepared to forgive him.

"Just a lot of work to do, Ma, nothing to worry about."

Her mother smiled as she slid the second *paratha* onto her plate. "Work should not be your life. Tomorrow night, I need you to be done with work by seven o'clock. I have someone I want you to have dinner with."

Nisha groaned. "Ma, now is not the time for a setup. I'm so not in the mood." She hadn't told her mother about Sameer. The pressure would be too much. Now that her mother had reconnected with Sameer's mother, Jhanvi, it wouldn't take long for the situation to spiral out of control. She could almost see the two mothers planning their wedding and walking her and Sameer toward the *mandap* before they even realized what was going on. As a young girl, marrying Sameer was all she had dreamed about. But now she didn't know what she wanted. Since she couldn't have children, there was no biological clock ticking in her head. But she did want a partner, someone to share her life with. Was Sameer that someone?

She and Sameer had barely gotten back together and already they were in a massive disagreement. Her mother had once told her that strong emotions came from a place of deep love. *A person does not react strongly to someone they don't care about.*

"You'll be happy with this one, I promise."

Nisha turned her attention back to her mother. She wished she could be honest but there was already so much pressure on her and Sameer's relationship, she didn't need the added stress that came with involving an overeager mother.

"Ma, please. I can't."

"You made a *vada* on the head of Lord Ganesh that you would attend a dinner whenever I asked you, and not be late. I'm holding you to that."

Nisha groaned. She'd forgotten about the deal she'd made with her mother and regretted it more than ever. "Fine, Ma, I'll be home by seven."

Her mother shook her head. "Not home. You go to the Mahal hotel. We are having dinner with Sameer and his parents."

Twelve

Her mother looked at her appraisingly when they met in the lobby of the Mahal hotel. *Was it just a week ago that I was leaving this lobby in a town car after having mind-blowing sex with Sameer?* She'd tried texting him to ask if he could skip the dinner. She couldn't because she had made a promise to her mother but maybe he would be decent enough to respect her wishes. She couldn't believe that her mother had planned this dinner. *Surely Ma isn't setting me up with Sameer?* That would be both hilarious and frightening.

On top of that, she was nervous about seeing his parents. Jhanvi Singh hated Nisha, a fact that her mother didn't know. When they were in college,

Jhanvi often accused her of enabling Sameer's bad behaviors by covering for him. Just because they were family friends, Jhanvi expected Nisha to be Sameer's keeper and babysitter.

"You need more lipstick."

Nisha sighed and opened her purse to apply more gloss. She didn't have any fight left in her. Her mother had looked disapprovingly at the business suit Nisha had chosen to wear. It was the same one she'd worn to work earlier that morning. Today had been another grueling day at the office. Contrary to Jessica's predictions, a large department store wanted to meet with her right away for some exclusive designs. Nisha had texted Jessica to let her know that she planned to talk to Sameer's father directly at the dinner tonight to ask him to intervene and let Jessica back. Her friend had been excited for her success but let her know that she had gotten her old job back and was happy to be getting a steady paycheck. Nisha knew that even if she came up with the money to get rid of the Mahal Group, she'd never get her friend back, and for that she didn't know how to forgive Sameer.

Intellectually she knew it wasn't completely Sameer's fault, but she couldn't help wishing that he'd stood up for her. How could she think of him as a life partner when he couldn't even be a loyal business partner?

As they rode the elevator in silence, her heart was stretched into an overwhelming number of emotions: excitement at seeing Sameer again, apprehension for how she'd feel in his presence, dread that he'd taken her text seriously and would skip dinner. When the elevator doors opened, her heart soared but her stomach clenched to see Sameer standing there. He was dressed in a black suit with a light blue shirt and an open collar. He looked dashingly handsome as always and she felt warmth deep in her belly. No matter how many times she lectured herself, she'd never get him out of her system.

He reached down and touched his mother's feet. *Pairi Pauna.* The traditional way of greeting elders. Her mother put her hand on his head and wished him a long life. Sameer's parents, Dharampal and Jhanvi, were right behind him. She likewise touched their feet. It had been a long time since she'd followed that tradition and it made her nostalgic for India. While there were many things she loved about living in America, the closeness of the friendships and family in India was something she missed every day.

Jhanvi was impeccably dressed in a turquoise silk tunic, silky black pants and diamond solitaire earrings. She eyed Nisha's clothes and she suddenly wished she had put on something a little dressier. His father was dressed in a black suit with a maroon turtleneck underneath. Behind them stood Sameer's sister Divya, looking beautiful in a simple black dress.

Her mother hugged Sameer's mother. The two women held on tightly to each other and Nisha suddenly realized why her mother had gotten back in touch with her old friend. Her mother had left everything behind for Nisha: her home, her friends. Nisha didn't need her as much anymore and it was time her mother got back to having her own life.

Divya stepped forward and hugged Nisha. Sameer's sister was petite with long dark hair and dark eyes.

"Is your fiancé here?" Nisha asked. She still couldn't believe that Sameer's parents were not only supporting Divya's unorthodox career, but also her marrying an American man.

Divya shook her head. "He had a meeting in LA that he couldn't miss."

Nisha had a million questions for Divya but Jhanvi interrupted. "Come sit, chai and *pakoras* are ready. Nisha, I remember how much you love my little cucumber sandwiches so I made them myself."

In India, it was common to serve chai with appetizers and dessert. Nisha smiled warmly at Sameer's mother. "Thank you, Auntie, I have missed your sandwiches." She'd forgotten about the cucumber and mint chutney sandwiches that had been a staple of her childhood.

Nisha eyed the sofa where she and Sameer had made love just a week ago. So little time had passed yet there was so much distance between them. Sameer touched her back lightly and she knew without looking at him that he was thinking the same thing. There was an indelible connection between them.

"Actually, Ma, do you mind if Nisha and I take our chai and food to the office? We have some business to discuss."

Jhanvi and her mother exchanged looks that made Nisha uncomfortable. *What are these ladies up to?* "Of course, I am sure you have a lot to talk about," her mother said. Sameer's mother went about making them plates and pouring cups of chai. Nisha didn't want to be alone with Sameer, even for a second. She didn't trust herself with him. But if they didn't talk things through, something would explode in front of their parents and that was a scene she didn't want.

Sameer led her through the kitchen to a door in the back that she hadn't noticed before. There was a chef in the kitchen cooking up a storm. It smelled like garlic and ginger and a heady mix of spices. Nisha realized that she'd skipped lunch again and her stomach rumbled. The office was very small in contrast to the generous space of the kitchen and great room. The desk took up most of the space and there were two guest chairs. It was entirely too small for her and Sameer to be in here together. She could smell his cologne, feel the heat coming off his body, and it was too much for her. The anger was already dissipating and she couldn't have that. It was how he always reeled her in.

They set their plates on the little round table between the chairs. Nisha kept the chai cup in her hand to keep something between her and Sameer.

She stared at Sameer. He had requested the meeting. He could break the ice.

"Listen, I tried my best to make Arjun understand about Jessica but he's unmovable when it comes to business. Regardless of her intentions, what she did was not just wrong but illegal. Arjun wanted to press criminal charges."

Nisha choked on the sip of tea she'd just taken. "Don't you dare. She was never going to keep the money…"

Sameer held up a hand. "I convinced him not to. Jessica would never get a job in finance with something like that on her record. She's your friend and I didn't want to ruin her career. I got him to back off that notion."

Nisha breathed a sigh of relief but she couldn't bring herself to thank him. He could've done more to make sure it hadn't come to the point where Jessica had to leave the business.

She glared at him and continued drinking her tea. She needed the hot liquid to cool down the anger bubbling through her.

"Also, Arjun is lending Vinod to you to do the operational and financial management and hire another manager."

"Excuse me? Who asked you to do that? I will handle the finances until *I* hire someone else. Vinod has done enough. I don't need him hovering over me."

Sameer took a breath. "You're going to have a

lot of orders coming in over the next few months. You're the talent. *Nisha* cannot succeed without you designing the clothes. Someone else needs to handle the finances, order materials, send out shipments. You can't be bogged down with stuff like that."

He was right, of course. Jessica had only been gone a week and already Nisha was feeling overwhelmed with all that she had to do.

"Let me think about it," she said evasively. She knew there were few choices but she really didn't like the idea of letting Vinod interfere even more than he already had.

Suddenly it seemed to take too much effort to stand. She sat on one of the chairs and set down her cup of tea. Sameer grabbed one of the mini cucumber sandwiches from the plate, knelt down before her and lifted his hand to her mouth. His eyes looked pleadingly at her.

"Nisha, we are going to have disagreements. But haven't we grown up? Can't we separate the business from personal?"

She stayed quiet. He had a point but she wasn't ready to let go of her anger.

"Look," he continued, "my brother and I disagree on a lot. We argue, we fight, we threaten to sue each other, but at the end of the day, we break naan together because we're family. If you and I are going to be together, we need to do the same thing. *Nisha* is your business. It's not who you are and it doesn't define our relationship."

"*Nisha* is my life, and if we're going to make our relationship work, I need for the Mahal Group to get out of my company as soon as we can pay back the loan."

He nodded. "I will make that happen. Look, I know you hate Vinod but the kid is a master negotiator. He'll get you good contracts on your upcoming orders and my guess is that you'll be able to buy us out within six months."

She blew out a breath and nodded. He widened his eyes into that puppy-dog look that melted her heart, and her resolve crumbled into pieces. He touched the cucumber sandwich to her lips and she opened her mouth wide and gently bit him as she took the little sandwich into her mouth.

He smiled. "Now that's what I'm talking about." He leaned closer to her. "What else would you like to bite?"

She could think of several choice responses as he closed the distance between them. She gently nipped his ear. "You know I hate you."

He smiled. "You hate that you can't resist me."

He knows me so well.

She leaned forward and grabbed his lower lip with her teeth. He put his hand on her cheek and returned the kiss. It was warm and sensual and filled her with longing for him. She had overreacted. After all, Jessica had done something she shouldn't have. Had Vinod done what Jessica had, she'd be the first to make sure he went to jail. Sameer was right. She'd let her friendship with Jessica cloud her business sense.

"Did I tell you that I have fantasies of you in this business suit? It's what you were wearing the first time I walked into your studio."

"Oh yeah?" she breathed. "Tell me about them."

He put his hand on her knee and worked his way up her leg. Her pantyhose had run earlier in the day so she'd taken them off and the feel of his hand on her bare thighs sent delicious sensations all through her body. He reached her grandma panties and she wished she'd worn something sexier. He didn't seem to care. He pushed them aside.

"Hmm, I see I'm having an effect on you."

She wanted his touch so badly, she couldn't stand it. He complied by putting a finger inside her. How could his simple touch make her want to explode? Now that she had him, how was she ever going to let him go?

A knock on the door jarred them both. Sameer stood quickly, grabbing a paper from the desk to hide the obvious bulge in his pants. Nisha had barely pulled down her skirt when Divya opened the door and peeked in. Nisha's face went hot as Divya's eyes raked over both of them.

"Oops, sorry, didn't mean to interrupt." Nisha was grateful that it was Divya and not Sameer's mother who had found them but Divya's face was pinched. "Dinner is ready. Come."

Nisha stood on shaky legs. *What am I thinking?*

Both their mothers were sitting right outside. She'd be mortified if Sameer's mother had caught them in a compromising position. As it was, she was sure she and Sameer had enough guilt on their faces for Jhanvi to surmise what they'd been doing.

As they made their way to the dining table, Divya tapped her arm. "Once dinner is done, can I talk to you?" Nisha didn't like the seriousness of her voice but she nodded.

The dining room table had been set with fancy china plates, crystal glasses, a maroon-and-gold table runner and fresh flowers. A woman in a sari went around the table filling the glasses from a pitcher of ice water. Nisha smiled as she remembered that Sameer's mother always traveled with an army of maids. There was a time her mother had done the same. Back when her parents were maintaining the illusion of a happy marriage.

Sameer's mother directed everyone to their seats. Nisha and Sameer were seated across from each other, with Sameer's father at the head of the table and Sameer's mother on the opposite end. Her mother was next to Nisha, and Divya was next to Sameer. The menu for tonight was Indo-Chinese and Nisha was pleasantly surprised. You could get almost any type of cuisine in New York but good Indo-Chinese was hard to find. The sari-clad ladies ladled hakka noodles onto her plate and she breathed in the aroma. The lo mein–style noodles were stir-fried with bell peppers, onions and Indian spices. They were complemented with chili chicken that was like a spicy General Tso's.

"Oh my God, I haven't had hakka noodles and chili chicken for years!" Nisha exclaimed. In fact, the last time might have been in college.

"Sameer told me that you would eat this for lunch every day in college," Jhanvi said.

Nisha gave him a smile and thanked his mother but she was starting to get suspicious at why all her favorite things had been made for this dinner. Especially knowing how Sameer's mother felt about her. *You are a smart girl, Nisha. Why don't you encourage him to be more serious about his studies and stop him from partying?* Back then, she'd longed to tell his mother that she couldn't control Sameer any better than his parents could but her Indian sensibilities had kept her from speaking rudely to an elder.

"I am so happy to see you again, Nisha. It has been a long time and you've grown into a fine young woman. I hear you are also a successful businesswoman and top designer," Dharampal said.

Nisha thanked Sameer's father politely and could feel her mother beaming next to her. Indian parents considered the success of their children as a marker of their own achievements.

"The boys must be lining up with *rishtas* for her," Jhanvi remarked.

Nisha caught Sameer's eye and he grinned at her. Normally conversations like this would have her awkwardly changing the topic but the look Sameer gave her warmed her heart. *Did he talk to his parents about us? Is his mother about to broach our* rishta *with Ma?* The prospect both excited and scared her. She needed more time to make sure that what she and Sameer had was real. Despite their long friendship, they hadn't spent enough time getting to know each other as mature adults. It had only been an hour ago that she'd wanted nothing to do with him. Their relationship was too volatile to make a commitment right now. On the other hand, perhaps an engagement would give them the freedom they needed to be together. Her mother would get off her back and she and Sameer could spend quality time together cementing their relationship. A long engagement might be the pressure test they needed.

"A lot of boys are interested but Nisha is very selective," her mother commented diplomatically.

Their mothers were talking about them as if they weren't in the room. Sameer smirked and Nisha smiled at the expression on his face.

"Don't I know it. Sameer has been the same way with girls." His mother looked at her son. "But now that he and Nisha have reconnected, I'm hoping all that will change."

Here it comes.

"I am so grateful that you invested in Nisha's business. She absolutely refused to marry until her label launched," Reeta said.

Jhanvi looked pointedly at Nisha. "I am ready for Sameer to be married and I can't think of a better girl than Nisha." She gave them both an eager smile and went on. "He is a new man now. He's serious about being involved in the family business and I think settling down with a wife like Nisha is the next step in his life."

Nisha had dreamed of this moment all through college. She'd pictured it almost exactly as it was unfolding now. Except the excitement she'd pictured on Sameer's face, and the bubble of joy in her own heart, was missing.

"Ma, don't you think it's a little soon?" The words from Sameer hit Nisha right in the gut. *He* had doubts? She caught his eye but his expression was unreadable. "Don't get me wrong. I adore Nisha, but I'm not ready for marriage."

He *adored* her?

Divya chimed in. "Ma, Sameer needs to focus on himself right now. Marriage is not good for him."

Divya gave her mother a pointed look and Nisha's stomach clenched. *What am I missing here?* While she'd never been that close to Divya, she thought Divya liked her.

"You children think you know everything. Your father and I, and Reeta, are more experienced than you. There is no getting ready for marriage. Having a wife is what Sameer needs to settle down and become responsible."

So I'm supposed to be a literal ball and chain for him?

Her mother chimed in. "You two children have

known each other for so many years. You have gone through so much together. It's time you do something positive in your life. Marriage is the natural next step, no?"

Before she could tell her mother that there was no rush, Sameer spoke up. "Auntie, I have a lot of respect for you and for Nisha but I just can't think about marriage right now."

He wouldn't meet her eyes. The hakka noodles that had smelled so good just a few minutes ago now made her want to throw up. An awkward silence settled over the table. Finally, Divya broke it. "Well, since the mothers clearly have wedding fever, why don't we talk about mine."

"Are you sure you won't run away from this one? I had to chase you down last time, remember," Sameer said with forced humor.

Divya stuck her tongue out at Sameer and he turned to Nisha. His mouth was saying one thing but his eyes were begging her to understand. *Understand what? That nothing has changed in the last eight years? You still don't want to commit to me.* "The short story is that Divya was engaged to this nice but snooze of a guy, Vivek. She couldn't bring herself to break the engagement so on the day of her wedding, she's sitting at the *mandap* and this random white guy shows up claiming he loves her. She runs away with him. Like picks up her skirt and hauls ass. Arjun and I had to chase them down the streets of Vegas."

Nisha couldn't help but smile. "Was that Ethan? Were you dating at the time?"

Divya shook her head. "It was Ethan, but I had no idea who he was at the time. He meant to crash his ex-girlfriend's wedding and came to the wrong one. I saw it as a sign and convinced him to run with me."

Divya went on to tell her how the rest of it had transpired. Nisha had not heard the full story before and found herself relaxing despite the emotions raging through her.

After dinner, Jhanvi asked them to come to the sitting area for chai and dessert. Nisha wanted nothing more than to go home. As they stood, Divya cornered her. "Do you mind if we have a chat?" Nisha nodded and Divya led her to the office where less than an hour ago she and Sameer had been.

Divya closed the door and turned to Nisha. "I apologize for getting right to the point, especially since we haven't had a chance to catch up, but I want to talk to you before the oldies want us back."

Nisha braced herself.

"You know that Sameer got out of rehab around ten months ago?" Nisha nodded and Divya continued. "I know he cares for you but you need to know that his therapist at the rehab center advised him not to get involved with anyone for minimum a year, preferably more"

Nisha's mouth went dry. "Why not?"

Divya sighed. "There are many reasons, but the most important one you should know about is that addicts have a tendency to replace one addiction with another."

"So you think I'm an addiction?"

Divya shifted on her feet. "No. The point is that he needs to be self-reliant, focus on himself, not become dependent on you. I also worry that being with you will remind him of the bad times. He blames himself for the accident. I don't want this relationship to stress him to the point where he has a relapse."

Nisha's stomach roiled. She wanted to tell Divya that she was wrong, that she didn't understand their relationship, but she couldn't.

"You don't have anything to worry about. As you heard at dinner, Sameer is not interested in marriage."

"He might not want to get married tomorrow but it was obvious to anyone at that table that there is a lot between you two." She took a breath. "Look, I would like nothing more than for you and Sameer to be together. But I'm asking, no, begging, please cool it off with him. He needs more time. If he's not doing this for the right reasons, he's going to end up back in the same dark place he just recovered from."

Tears stung Nisha's eyes. The last thing she wanted to do was jeopardize his sobriety. What if Divya was right? What if this whole time she had just been one of the amends that Sameer was making?

Sameer knocked on the door and Divya let him

in. "I'll try to keep the mothers at bay and give you two time to talk."

"Hey, I knew my mom put Arjun up to investing in your business but I didn't know that she was scheming with your mother to plan our wedding."

Nisha nodded. "Me neither, though I should've figured it out. She's been desperate for me to get married."

He shook his head. "Marriage is so far from what I want right now."

Divya's words were still rolling around in her mind. "Not now, but eventually you want to get married, right?"

He shrugged. "Maybe. But why are we talking about this? I thought you wanted to focus on your label, and marriage isn't something you want anyway."

She looked away. *What do I want?* If there was anything the last few years had taught her, it was the pain and suffering marriage caused. Having a front row seat to her parent's marriage, she didn't see the point it in, especially if she wasn't going to have children. "You're right, I do want to concentrate on my label."

"Then there's no issue. We've been together for like two minutes. Let's take it one day at a time."

She nodded but her stomach was in knots. He was using the same appeasing tone he used to use with the college girls when they asked him when he would call them. As irrational as it was, while she questioned the institution of marriage, it bugged her that he didn't want it. She'd seen him get infatuated with a girl and then distance himself when the lust burned out. What if that was happening with her?

They returned to the sitting room where *ras malai* was being served. Nisha was handed a bowl of the cottage cheese balls soaked in sweet cardamom-flavored milk. She had no appetite. Her mother was sitting on the couch opposite to the one where she and Sameer had made love the night before. She took a seat next to her mother.

"Nisha, I was just telling your mother that we are throwing a dinner party for Hema next week."

Sameer spoke up. "Hema, as in Arjun's ex-fiancée?"

His mother nodded and turned toward Nisha and her mother. "Arjun had been engaged to this lovely girl, Hema. Actually, Reeta you should remember her parents. Aparna and Mukesh Dharav. They were at many of our parties."

Her mother stiffened and Nisha felt her own body tense. *It can't be. This has to be a coincidence.*

Nisha set down her plate and grabbed her mother's hand. Jhanvi went on. "Well, Arjun fell in love with Rani and broke the engagement. We were so embarrassed, especially because Mukesh invested in our business to allow our expansion into North America, and then you heard the story about Divya. So, we thought, why not set up Hema with Vivek."

Divya burst out laughing. "Ma, only you would set up the people this family has jilted. I'm surprised they even agreed to come."

Jhanvi shot her daughter a dark look.

Her mother's hand had gone ice-cold. Jhanvi turned to them. "As I was saying, I'd love it if you both came as well. I'm also inviting a few of the prominent Indian families in the city. It's time you and Nisha entered the right social circles again."

If her mother's body had been tense before, now it was like a rock. Nisha's own stomach was in a thousand knots. Was she reading her mother's body language incorrectly? Then another thought hit her. "Auntie, did you say that Hema was Arjun's fiancée? Does that mean she's his age?"

Her mother squeezed Nisha's hand warningly but Nisha ignored her.

Jhanvi frowned at the non sequitur question. "No, she's much younger than Arjun. Younger than Sameer too. Twenty-five or maybe twenty-six now."

"How many children do the Dharavs have?"

"Just two, a son and a daughter." Jhanvi was frowning at Nisha's sudden interest in the family.

The puzzle pieces fell into place for Nisha. Her father had an affair with a woman whom she met at a party. The woman's husband was wealthy and powerful, which was why her father refused to divulge who she was. It was only because Nisha had overhead his conversation the night before the accident that she knew the woman her father had a thirty-year affair with was named Aparna. Also, her father and the woman named Aparna had a daughter twenty-six years ago whom Aparna had passed off as her husband's.

"We would love to come to your party, Auntie," Nisha replied.

Thirteen

"Nisha, why are you going?" her mother asked pleadingly.

They'd already had this conversation at least five times, with her mother begging, reasoning, and threatening her not to go but Nisha was unmoved.

"Because I need answers and you and Dad are never going to give them to me."

"We don't even know if it's the same Aparna."

"Which is why I'm going to the party tonight, to find out." Nisha had little doubt in her mind that Aparna was her father's mistress and Hema was her half-sister. Her mother's reaction had given her away. Her mother knew much more than she shared.

Nisha had lived in the awkward space of lies and

pretense all her life and she was tired of it. She had watched her mother pine for her father's love, soaking in the dribbles he offered. Her mother claimed that she stayed for Nisha's sake but deep down she knew her mother was in love with her father. But why did Aparna continue the affair for so long? Why weren't these women able to move on? Why did they continue to love a man who wouldn't commit to either one of them?

"What are you going to do?"

"I'm going to talk to her, ask her if she knows Dad and see how she reacts."

"What will all this accomplish? How will this make things better?"

Nisha didn't have an answer to that. She just knew that she needed to meet the woman who had ruined her childhood and her relationship to her father. She needed to understand why her mother and Aparna couldn't move on, what they got from loving a man who wasn't a hundred percent theirs. Her mother couldn't articulate the reason why, perhaps Aparna could.

She applied a final coat of mascara and checked her appearance in the mirror. She had altered one of her dresses to fit her for tonight's dinner. It was a one-shoulder silhouette in jet-black. The dress fell below the knee in a diagonal cut and was belted at the waist with a thick silver chain.

Sameer picked her up, thankfully not on his motorcycle. She got into the back seat of the town car. He was dressed in his standard black suit and smelled just as great as he looked.

"You know you could've just sent the car, or I could've taken an Uber," she told him.

The driver pulled out into traffic suddenly, making her slide in the seat. Sameer pulled her against him. "And miss spending these minutes alone with you?"

"We're not alone." She looked pointedly at the driver.

"He's focused on driving," Sameer said, nibbling her neck, "and you look way too good for me to keep my hands off you."

He moved his lips down her neck to her bare shoulder and her body lit up. They'd seen each other a few times for dinner during the week but his parents were staying in the penthouse and she had her mother at home so they hadn't been able to be with each other. Sameer had suggested getting a hotel room in the city but Nisha refused. She wanted a break from their physical relationship to see if there was more than just lust between them. She'd enjoyed their dinners together where they spent hours talking. She'd learned that Sameer hadn't just gone back and completed college but he'd also spent the pandemic getting an online executive MBA. Their family empire had expanded and Arjun was already handing him the New York hotel to manage. They'd gotten to know each other all over again and it was beautiful, but also frightening. She was more connected to him than ever. If things didn't work out between them, how would she ever move on? Would she end up like her mother and Aparna, in love with a man who couldn't love her back?

Nisha debated whether to tell Sameer what she suspected about Aparna and Hema. Her mother had warned her that she couldn't play with their family's *izzat*. In Indian communities, reputation was everything.

Can I trust Sameer?

As if sensing the shift in her mood, he stopped kissing her and put his arm around her.

"What's the matter?"

"There's no great way to say this so I'll just spit it out. I think Aparna Dharav is the woman my father's been having an affair with."

Sameer's eyes widened. "Are you sure?"

She nodded. "There's more." Her throat was completely dry. Other than her mother and father, no one else knew that her father had a daughter with his mistress. Revealing that fact would ruin the entire Dharav family. She had no idea how much Mukesh Dharav knew about the affair, and she seriously doubted he knew about Hema. She hadn't slept a wink all night wondering how she would feel if someone told her that she was not her father's daughter.

"Outside of my immediate family, you are the only person who's about to know that my father had a daughter with his mistress."

Sameer's eyes widened. "Hema?" He sat back in the seat.

"Mukesh Dharav knows about the affair but I don't think he knows about the daughter."

"Indian families are good at keeping secrets but I'm pretty sure that Hema doesn't know and neither does her father."

"How can you be so sure?"

"When her and Arjun's *rishta* was finalized, her parents put, like, a billion dollars into the Mahal hotel group. No offense, but you know how it is, there's no way her father would put in that kind of money if there was any doubt that she was his." Sameer paused. "I know this has got to be torture for you but be very careful. If there's even a one percent chance you're wrong, a whisper of your suspicions can ruin a lot of relationships."

He was right. How sure was she? *Pretty sure.* If she'd had any doubts, her mother begging her not to go to the party and her own refusal to do so were telltale signs.

"Why does it matter who your father's mistress is?"

It was a good question, one that Nisha didn't have an answer to. All she knew was that she had spent a lot of time googling every Aparna in India—there were hundreds of thousands—to try and figure out who her father's mistress was. She could understand if her father had an affair with a woman but he hadn't just had an affair with Aparna. He had a decades-long relationship with her. How did they continue like that? She hoped that talking to Aparna could give her some level of closure.

The party hadn't started when they arrived. The guests were running on IST—Indian Standard Time.

Divya greeted them at the door. "Wow, you look amazing. Is that one of your designs?"

Nisha nodded. "You know, I never did thank you for coming up with the idea of investing in South Asian artists. That's a really wonderful thing to do."

Divya beamed. "I can't take all the credit. Rani is also an artist and we realized that South Asian children are really discouraged from pursuing careers in the arts so we want to support them."

"I think it's a great program and if I'm successful, I'll happily contribute."

"Not if, when," Sameer chimed in.

"Do the parental units know that you two are together?" Divya whispered. Sameer shook his head. "I'd rather not tell them quite yet."

Nisha looked at her shoes. The conversation with Divya wasn't far from her mind. "That's a smart move but if you don't want them to find out, I suggest you stop looking at her like she's a *gulab jamun* you want to pop in your mouth."

Sameer play-punched his sister's arm but he did move away from her as the elevator dinged. Without being introduced, she knew it was the Dharav family. It wasn't anything specific but more of a feeling when she looked at the younger woman. She moved away as Jhanvi appeared and greeted them.

When Nisha was introduced to the Dharavs, she watched them closely.

"Nisha is Reeta and Anil Chawla's daughter," Jhanvi said. Nisha's eyes were on Aparna and the last one percent doubt she had vanished. The panic in Aparna's eyes was evident as she searched the room.

"My parents aren't here," Nisha said as Aparna's eyes landed on her. The other woman's relief was palpable.

Jhanvi moved them along into the great room, where appetizers were being served by tuxedoed waiters. Additional guests arrived and Nisha met a lot of people whose names she would never remember. The only thing she could focus on all evening was studying Hema and Aparna. Hema was a beautiful woman, nearly as tall as Nisha, with fair skin, long straight hair and eyes that lit up her face. She was dressed in an elegant maroon dress that showed off her enviable body.

"You know, I've been admiring your dress all night. I'm Hema."

Nisha forced herself not to betray the panic that rose up her throat when she turned and looked at Hema close-up. Hema had her father's distinctive chin with a little dimple in the middle. She was looking at her half-sister. As an only child, she'd dreamed of what it would be like to have siblings, wondered whether her lonely childhood would have been more tolerable with a sister with whom she could share clothes and secrets. Had she latched onto Sameer all those years ago because she'd been so lonely?

Sameer stepped beside her. "You are looking at the next Vera Wang or Coco Chanel. Nisha designed this dress and just had a show a few days ago."

Hema's eyes widened. "Wow, that is amazing." She leaned forward. "It's my dad's sixtieth birthday next month and my mom and I are throwing him this grand party in Dubai. Any chance you'd consider designing something for me?"

Nisha's mouth felt like she'd eaten mud.

"She's not cheap, you know," Sameer said lightly.

Hema laughed. "For a dress like that, I'll pay whatever you ask."

Nisha opened the silver clutch purse she was carrying. Most women stuffed their evening bags with makeup, their cell phone, maybe a tampon. Her purse was full of business cards. She handed one to Hema now. "Call or email me. Let's set up a time to discuss what you want. It would be my honor to design for you."

"Let me introduce you to my mom. I bet she'll want an outfit too."

Hema walked off to get her mother and Nisha stood rooted to the floor. "Her chin, the way she talks with her hands. It's just like my dad," she said to Sameer.

He squeezed her hand. "Do you want to talk to Aparna privately?"

Nisha nodded. Whatever it was she had come here to do, she had to do it privately. Hema seemed like a nice girl who didn't deserve to have her world turned upside down.

"Go wait in the office. I'll get her," Sameer said.

He navigated his way through the now-crowded room and Nisha made her way to the little office. What would she even say to Aparna? *So you're the bitch that ruined mine and my mother's lives. Can you tell me why?*

It seemed like forever but finally the door opened and Aparna walked in. She thanked Sameer and then looked at Nisha. She wanted Sameer to stay but knew that Aparna wouldn't be as forthcoming in his presence.

The two women stared at each other for a long time. Aparna broke the silence. "I'm guessing by the way you're looking at me that you know who I am."

Nisha nodded and sank into the chair; she couldn't trust her legs to hold her up. Aparna did the same. She was dressed in an elegant black sari with copper-colored embroidery. She was a beautiful woman with stylish hair, a youthful face and an elegant grace. As beautiful as she was, though, she was about the same age as her mother, and nothing extraordinary. It clearly wasn't just lust that drove the affair.

"Your father told me that you've known for a few years."

Nisha nodded. "Is it still going on?"

Aparna shook her head. "I ended it a few years ago."

Right around the time her father had called her mother back to India.

"Why?"

Aparna sighed. "It wasn't one thing. Hema's engagement to Arjun had broken and I learned a lot about my daughter's hopes and dreams that I hadn't known. It made me realize that my double life had cost me closeness to my children. Then Mukesh found out and he gave me an ultimatum to choose your father or him."

Aparna paused like there was more to say but then fell silent.

Tears stung Nisha's eyes. Aparna had chosen her husband and family but her father had chosen Aparna.

"How did the affair start?"

Aparna looked pained. "There's no easy answer to that. Your father and I both went to school in Simla. I was in the girls' convent and he was in the boys' school. We met at a social function and fell in love. My mother died when I was a child and my father died while I was in school. My father extracted a dying promise from Mukesh's parents that they would marry him to me. Before Anil could do anything, I was married off to Mukesh. A year after I was wed to Mukesh, your father married your mother and I tried to forget about him.

Then we met at a party. When I saw your father, it was as if no time had passed. I was really unhappy in my own marriage and he provided comfort that I desperately needed."

"For almost thirty years?" Nisha failed to keep the disgust out of her voice.

"We hadn't planned it that way. I don't know when the days turned into months and the months into years. The familiarity of our friendship was what kept the affair going. It wasn't just a physical relationship. Most of the time we weren't even in the same city. For me it was about companionship, about sharing my life with someone who understood me, who truly cared about my happiness. We were a comfort to each other. To my husband I was just a trophy wife."

Comfort. The word left a nasty taste in her mouth. Aparna had used her father for comfort. Sameer had used her for comfort their first night together. Had she used him the same way for years? A balm for her loneliness. Had she confused friendship with love?

"Eight years ago, you wanted to run away with my father. What happened?"

Aparna looked down. "It was a bad time in my marriage and I ran to your father in desperation. He too was unhappy and we hatched a plan to start a new life together. Our children were grown and we felt that it was time to live for ourselves. It was stupid and careless. Your accident gave me time to cool down and realize that I couldn't do such a thing, my children still needed me."

"Is there any chance you'll restart the affair?"

She shook her head. "Once I ended it with your father, there was a new level of honesty between me and Mukesh, a fresh beginning. I'm giving my marriage a chance."

"Does Hema know?"

That got Aparna's attention. She looked wide-eyed at Nisha. "What about Hema?"

Nisha cocked her head. After baring her soul, was this woman really going to deny it?

"I know you and my father had a daughter. Hema has his chin."

Aparna leaned over and clasped Nisha's hands. "I know I have no right to ask you this but please don't say anything. Mukesh has no idea and neither does Hema."

So much for honesty with your husband.

"Your father refused to acknowledge Hema as his own. Mukesh would've divorced me and kept my son. Hema and I would've been on the streets and she'd be nothing as a bastard child. I had to do what was best for her."

And best for you. The more Aparna talked, the more disgusted Nisha became. Was this what marriage was supposed to be? Selfishness, secret children, lying spouses?

"Please, can you promise me that you won't tell

Hema? She adores her father. It will kill her to find this out."

Nisha nodded. She wouldn't wish her father on Hema. A man who had refused to claim his own daughter, and had forced his wife to stay with him just to save face in society.

"Nisha, I know you think I'm a horrible person but please understand that I was very young when I started the affair with your father. He's my first love and I can never stop loving him. I never meant to hurt you or your mother."

"I won't say anything to Hema because she's done nothing wrong and doesn't deserve to have her life turned upside down. But, I'd like to have a relationship with her, even if it's as a friend. I don't have any siblings and I don't think I can go through life pretending she doesn't exist."

Aparna pinched the bridge of her nose. Nisha stood. She was done with this conversation. She left the room and literally bumped into Sameer. It was clear he'd been outside the room waiting for her.

"Are you okay?"

She shook her head. "I need to get out of here."

They grabbed their coats and he escorted her out of the hotel. "I want to walk."

It was still early in the night and the city was alive. They walked in silence for a while. Sameer held her hand as she mulled over the conversation with Aparna in her head. *Comfort.* Was that all she had with Sameer? Was she hanging on to him because he was her first love, the way Aparna had done with her father?

They walked to Bryant Park. The grass had browned. Soon the main area would be turned into an ice rink and the winter village would be set up. They found a bench and sat down, and Sameer put his arm around her. She'd worn her winter wool coat, yet the fall air chilled her.

"I think she stayed with my father because he was familiar."

"She's been married to her husband for over thirty years. That's not enough to get familiar with him?"

Nisha chewed the inside of her cheek. "She never gave her marriage a chance. Her heart was always with my father." She thought about the men she had dated. She'd never gotten close to any of them. Was it because they weren't right for her, or was it because they weren't Sameer? Would she spend the rest of her life waiting for him to make a commitment?

"Where do we go next, Sameer? I mean with our relationship?"

"We're taking it a day at a time."

The days turned into months and the months into years.

She turned toward him so she could look him in the eyes. "I love you, Sameer. I always have and always will. Even when I hated you, it was because I loved you so much."

His breath caught. He opened his mouth to say something but she put a finger to his lips. Her throat was dry and she desperately wanted a bottle of water. *What am I doing?*

"I know you love me. You always have. But I don't want just the words. I want more."

Fourteen

Sameer looked up to see his sister enter his bedroom. Divya sat on the bed and tucked her feet beneath her. "It's a tie kind of day, huh?"

He nodded and restarted the knot. He detested wearing ties but he had an important meeting. Arjun had been giving him increasing responsibility for the New York hotel. While Sameer appreciated his brother's trust, it was also overwhelming. After their walk in the park the night before, Nisha hadn't wanted to go back to the party, so he'd driven her home. He'd come back to the hotel and stayed up until three in the morning poring over projections and contracts to get ready for a 6:00 a.m. Zoom meeting with their office in India. He was running on fumes, physically and emotionally.

"I am checking in to see how you're doing."

He loved his sister but despite being younger than him, she could be protective. "I'm doing fine, Div."

"You don't sound fine."

"That's because I barely slept for three hours and I'm focused on this meeting happening in thirty minutes." He hadn't meant to snap at his sister but his emotions were frayed.

Divya sighed. "Look, I'm leaving in a few hours to go meet up with Ethan in LA. Before I go, I want to know that you're going to be fine. If you're not ready to manage the hotel, just tell Arjun. If the relationship with Nisha is moving too fast, hit the pause button."

He turned to face her. "I know that my history doesn't give me a leg to stand on, but I need you to trust that I can handle it. I supported your relationship with Ethan. I need you to do the same for me and Nisha."

Divya pressed her lips together and gave him a small smile. She stood, kissed him on the cheek and gave him a long hug. He knew his sister meant well. She had been the one to get him to see the self-destructive path he was on and get him help.

He smiled at her. "I love Nisha. Always have, always will."

"Are you sure?" Divya shifted on the bed. "I

know you've been friends for a long time but you seem to be moving really fast."

"Says the woman who burned down the house to be with the love of her life."

She grinned. "I guess I don't have a leg to stand on either."

He tightened his tie then turned toward Divya. If there was one person who could understand his dilemma it was her. "Nisha wants a commitment."

"Are you ready for that?"

He sighed. "I don't have a doubt that I'll never love anyone the way I love her. But I'm not ready for marriage."

"Nisha will understand, she'll wait for you."

He nodded and bid farewell to Divya.

Nisha would wait as long as he asked her to. But was it fair to ask? He'd already put her through a lifetime of suffering, he couldn't put her through any more.

Nisha finished giving instructions to her new assistant, Lydia. It was past dusk yet the studio was buzzing with activity. Orders were pouring in and she'd been hiring new staff at a frenetic pace. She missed Jessica, who was doing well back at her old job. Sameer had convinced Vinod to subtract the money Jessica owed the business from the back pay Nisha owed her and close the matter of her embezzlement.

Nisha's phone buzzed with a message from Sameer. She asked him for a few more minutes and rushed into her office to finish getting dressed. It had been a week since she'd seen him last. Arjun had given him the reins of the New York hotel and her days were overflowing with work. They hadn't found time to see each other. They'd talked every day, though their calls were somewhat short. He hadn't brought up their conversation at the park and neither had she. It wasn't something she wanted to discuss over the phone. She had just put on her heels when Sameer walked through the front door.

He whistled when he saw her. "Tell me I can rip that dress off you later."

Nisha smiled. "Let's see how you behave tonight."

"Are you going to be okay in those heels?"

Nisha hated wearing heels but she had to get used to it. Since her show, there was a social invitation every weekend. Wearing her own creations was generating a lot of business and buzz. But most of her designs were meant to be worn with heels. She hadn't had time to design a few things for herself that she could wear with flats.

The driver of the town car was circling the block. It was rush hour and no one wanted to incur the wrath of commuters by idling in a driving lane. There were a lot of one-way streets in New York so they decided to walk a block and meet the driver on a street that was going Uptown.

Sameer held out his arm and she took hold. It felt good to be near him, to touch him. Had he thought about their conversation? Did he know what he wanted? Her stomach had been in knots the entire week. What if he asked her to wait? How long was she willing to give him?

Dammit! A searing-hot pain shot up her ankle and leg. Lost in thought as they exited the studio, she'd stepped into the pothole that she'd forgotten to avoid. Sameer grabbed onto her arm but her heel had broken and gotten stuck in a crack, and she fell onto her knees.

"Nisha!"

Of course, it had to be her bad leg where the heel had broken. The pain was intense and she didn't know what to do. Then Sameer was on the ground with her. He gently eased her foot out of the broken shoe and felt her leg. "Nothing feels broken. Do you feel pain when I touch your leg?"

She shook her head. "Nothing new. Just my ankle and the old injury."

"I'm going to pick you up. Let me know if you feel any sharp pain."

He picked her up, carrying her like a baby. She wrapped her arms around his neck. "Take me back into the studio and we'll figure something out."

He shook his head and began walking down the street. The town car was waiting for them at the corner of the next block, drawing the ire of everyone who was stuck in the traffic-jammed street.

Sameer instructed the driver to take them to the nearest emergency room or urgent care center.

"I think that's a little excessive," Nisha said, though at this point, the pain in her leg was so bad that her eyes were watering.

As luck would have it, there was an urgent care clinic two blocks from where they were. Once again Sameer carried her in. The nurse at the desk asked him to fill out some forms on a tablet but changed her mind when he glared at her and directed them to a room.

Sameer paced in the patient care room. They had been in the urgent care clinic for hours. A tech had taken X-rays of Nisha's foot, given her an ice pack and cleaned and bandaged the scrapes on her knees. Sameer's stomach churned seeing her lying on the bed with her foot raised, a white sheet on top of her. Her face was contorted in pain. Rationally he knew that this was just an accident but he couldn't help feeling as if he'd hurt her again. She wouldn't be in this much pain if it hadn't been for the accident.

The nurse asked whether Nisha wanted pain medication and she'd asked for ibuprofen. Asking for something stronger had been on his lips before he realized that he wasn't the patient.

Finally, the doctor walked through the door.

"Sorry for the wait, guys." The man was lean and tall with thick round glasses. "The good news is that nothing's broken, not even a hairline fracture."

"Then why is she in so much pain?"

He turned to Nisha. "You might have exacerbated your old injury, and sprained your ankle. We're going to put on a walking boot that will splint the ankle and help with the pain. I also recommend that you follow up with your orthopedist as soon as possible. He may need to do an MRI of your knee to make sure there isn't damage that we can't see just with an X-ray."

The knots in Sameer's stomach twisted tighter.

"Given your old injury, I recommend you take it easy for at least a couple of weeks, rest the leg as much as possible. Is there someone who can take care of you?"

Sameer stepped forward. "Don't worry, Doc. I'll take care of her."

As he said the words, his stomach turned. It was easy to makes promises but could he live up to them this time?

Sameer rubbed his neck as the elevator rose to the penthouse suites. It had been an exhausting two weeks since Nisha had injured her leg. Reeta Auntie had freaked out and insisted on caging Nisha in their condo. The MRI hadn't shown any additional issues but the orthopedist had suggested bed rest to make sure she didn't exacerbate her old injuries.

Just as the elevator doors dinged open, his mother FaceTimed him. He sighed.

"Yes, Ma!"

"You can be nicer to your mother."

"I'm tired, Ma. It's been a long day and I have to go down to Nisha's studio."

"How is her foot?"

"It's better. She can take the boot off tomorrow and if the orthopedist says it's okay, she'll be able to go back to her regular schedule."

"That's good. Reeta was telling me that you've been taking care of her company and her business is booming. Lots of work you are doing for her."

Nisha's company really had taken off. It had been a struggle to get her to rest but he didn't want her to injure her leg further by walking with the boot. He had finally convinced her to stay at home by personally going to the studio each day after he handled the hotel affairs to go over the books with Vinod and the production schedule with Lydia. While Lydia worked hard, she didn't have the maturity or experience to handle the volume of orders that were coming in.

More than a few times Nisha had mentioned how much easier things would be if Jessica was still there. While she and Nisha were still friends, he could sense that they weren't as close as they'd been. Was that just one more thing he'd screwed up for Nisha?

"I am looking out for our investment," he said in response to his mother's implied question.

"You think you can pull the wool over my eyes, but let me tell you. I am your mother. I know you've been dating Nisha since the moment you got back to New York."

He sighed. He knew it was nearly impossible to keep anything from his mother. "I have, Ma, but…"

"That's why I'm calling you." His mother held up a ring with a honking diamond on it. "I'm at the family jewelers and he showed this to me. It's an IF, E color, princess cut. Five carats. Nearly impossible to find. I'm going to get it for you to give to Nisha."

"Ma! I am nowhere near ready to propose to her."

"Why not? You have known her all your life. She is a good girl who has sorted out her life very well. She will be good for you."

"I have no doubt about that. But will I be good for her?"

"What do you mean?"

"Ma, I've been out of rehab less than a year. Now is not the time to put the added stress of a marriage on top of handling the New York hotel."

"This is exactly why you should get married. Nisha can help make sure you stay on the right track."

"That is not her job."

"It is if she's your wife. That's what wives do for their husbands."

"Keep them in line?"

He'd said it facetiously but his mother responded in a serious tone. "Yes! How do you think your father built this empire? How do you think Arjun has expanded the business? It is the women that give their husbands the strength to do what they must."

"Ma, all in good time. Why don't you focus on Divya's wedding?"

"Because I am not worried about her."

What went unsaid between them was that his mother had a lot of angst about him. His family was waiting with bated breath for him to fail, to slip back into his old ways. He was still a child to them. They'd let him walk on his own but were hovering nearby to catch him if he fell. Not if, *when* he fell. But he wasn't going to fall this time. There was nothing that would jeopardize his sobriety. Not even Nisha.

Fifteen

The orders were rolling in faster than even Vinod could process. Nisha's little studio was brimming with junior designers, assistants and seamstresses. She hated seeing Vinod in what she still thought of as Jessica's office but she had to admit that he knew what he was doing. He'd negotiated some pretty lucrative contracts. Just today, she had authorized a wire transfer to pay off her father's investment, and in a few months, she could pay back the Mahal Group, though getting the Mahal Group out of her life didn't seem as important now.

Sameer had been working tirelessly the last month. Though her boot had come off two weeks ago, he still came to the studio every day to work with Vinod, and to make sure she went home at a reasonable hour. She was amazed at how involved he stayed in the finances of her business while still running the hotel. The old Sameer would have caved under the pressure. Instead, he was not only managing her business but had grown it exponentially. Tonight, he'd gotten her invited to one of the most exclusive magazine parties. It was her opportunity to interact with the real power behind the fashion industry.

They hadn't talked about their conversation at the park but she no longer needed him to make some grand gesture to convince her that he'd commit to her. He'd already done it. The way he'd taken care of her over the last month showed her just how much he loved her, and that he had changed.

She checked her watch and waved to Vinod as she left to go back to her place to get dressed. She'd designed a special dress for the party. It was a short top, cropped just below the bra line, leaving her waist exposed. The long skirt was an Indian *lehngah* style but Westernized with a silk-cotton-blend fabric, detailing with buttons instead of embroidery, and a tighter skirt than what a *lehngah* typically allowed. While she no longer had to wear the boot, she didn't dare go back to heels. She had been outfitted with a pair of bland but necessary orthotic shoes which she made sure her skirt covered.

Sameer picked her up in the hotel town car. The party was at the magazine's Midtown offices and she belatedly realized that he had backtracked to pick her up. She should have taken an Uber and met him at the party. She kissed him on the cheek as she slid in beside him. His face was drawn.

"Are you sure you want to attend tonight? You look tired."

He nodded. "I'm beat, but this is an important night for you. I want to make sure you meet the right people."

She gave him another kiss on the cheek. "I'll have to pay you back for your generosity tonight. I told Ma that I was staying over at the hotel because the party was late and I didn't want to take an Uber late at night."

He gave her a small smile and nuzzled her neck. "Well, that might make it totally worthwhile to get dressed in this tux. You look great by the way." It still gave her a thrill to have him look at her like she was the most beautiful woman in the world.

He slipped his arm around her and his thumb brushed the exposed skin between her top and skirt and her body heated under his touch.

"Though you can give up the charade with your mother. My ma knows we're together. She called me on it a couple of weeks ago."

Nisha groaned. "How did she find out?"

He shrugged. "Divya knows, Vinod knows, which means Arjun knows and Rani knows. It was bound to get out."

She sat back, smiling. "The pressure's going to heat up for us to get engaged."

He sighed. "It already has. Ma has a ring picked out for you."

She eyed him. He didn't sound happy. In fact, he sounded weary.

"I don't want you to rush into anything you're not ready for," she said half-heartedly. The truth was that she was madly in love with him. Despite the fact that she saw him nearly every day, she wanted more. She wanted to wake up next to him each morning, see him at the end of the day and find out what he'd done. While she loved her mother, she was ready to move out and start a life of her own, share a house with Sameer. She was planning to ask him tonight if he wanted to tell their families they were dating but it seemed the cat was already out of the bag. His reaction, though, was not what she'd been hoping for.

He placed his hand on hers and squeezed. "I love you, but I want to make sure I'm on solid ground before we start a life together."

"What do you mean?"

He sighed. "I've just taken responsibility for the hotel, I need to focus on making it a success. Your label is going to explode in the next year or so, I don't want to distract you from that. Let's just enjoy each other right now, see where life takes us."

Her stomach clenched. He sounded like he was justifying distancing himself from her. Hadn't

Divya warned her that he wasn't ready for a relationship? Wasn't this what he did when things got tough or serious? He found excuses to justify running away.

He squeezed her hand. "You understand, don't you?"

We both have to finish college, figure out the rest of our lives. Now isn't the time for us to get involved. Let's forget about last night for now. We have such a nice friendship, let's not risk that. You understand what I'm saying, don't you?

The words he'd said eight years ago were etched in her memory. She nodded. She understood all too well.

Sameer had been to some glamorous parties in his lifetime, but the chic style of this magazine was something else. There was an eight-foot-tall ice sculpture of a woman posing in a floor-length gown. The magazine name and logo were prominent on the bottom of the skirt. High-top tables dressed in silver cloth and black accents were scattered around the room. Waiters walked around with an assortment of food and drinks. In the corners of the room, cages showed off scantily clad men and women dancing sensually. When they walked in, there was a literal red carpet where the press was allowed to take photos of the guests in front of a screen advertising the magazine name and logo. He hadn't been in the mood to come, but was glad he had now that he saw there was press coverage.

He let Nisha walk the red carpet alone. He didn't want the society pages to talk about him next to her picture. The focus should be on *Nisha* alone. He'd had enough publicity to last him a lifetime.

"There you are!" He'd been lost in his thoughts when Nisha caught up to him. She had a glass of champagne in her hand but she set it down as soon as she saw him.

"Can you believe this party?"

He smiled. "It's pretty spectacular."

"We should take a picture in front of that ice sculpture. Ma will die when she sees it. How did they even get that thing in here?"

He took a picture with her in front of the sculpture. They'd been standing for all of thirty seconds when the magazine's editor-in-chief approached her.

His phone buzzed and he stepped away to answer it. It was the hotel and Sameer dreaded whatever issue had come up now.

"Sameer Singh here."

He could barely hear the guy on the other end so he stepped out onto the terrace. It was cold but there was just enough warmth from the patio heaters to make it comfortable. He barely saw the Midtown view as he noticed there was a bar at the end of the terrace.

"Sir, I'm sorry to bother you this late, but we have an issue."

Sameer closed his eyes. He was exhausted and not in any mood to handle whatever guest drama was happening. It was endless. Guests were constantly upset because their room was too small, too cold, too hot or too white. Staff threatened to strike or sue every time a guest misbehaved with them; the rising costs of everything from toilet paper to alcohol made his balance sheets impossible; chefs threw tantrums because he wouldn't let them buy hundred-dollar steaks for a dish he could only charge sixty dollars for. Everyone expected miracles from him.

"Sir, New York City police are here and want to search the room of one of our guests. We haven't been able to raise the guest on the phone."

Sameer rolled his eyes. There were well-written procedures for this and he was irritated at the manager for calling him.

"Do they have a warrant?"

"Yes, sir. But..."

"But what? If they have a warrant then let them search the room. Don't have them sitting in the lobby where all of the guests can see them and freak out. Make sure you escort them through the service elevator, watch and document everything they do, and get them out as soon as possible."

"Yes, sir."

He hung up the phone feeling frustrated and tired.

A waiter appeared carrying tumblers of whiskey. Sameer eyed the tray. He wasn't addicted to alcohol. Technically he could drink if he wanted to. It might help him take the edge off the evening. He picked up a tumbler from the tray and took a deep breath of the malty, woodsy aroma. It wasn't the good stuff but it smelled comforting.

"Hi, I'm Aidan Matthews." Sameer looked up to find a tall, blond man holding out his hand. He'd been so focused on the whiskey, he hadn't notice him approach. The guy had a firm handshake but not the bone-crushing kind that men who were trying to compensate for something tended to give. Sameer tried to place him but couldn't. It wasn't that unusual. He met a lot of people at parties and at the hotel.

"Sameer Singh."

"I know. I saw you come in with Nisha Chawla. Your family owns the Mahal Group, right?"

Now Sameer was intrigued. "Yes."

"I'm glad you invested in *Nisha*. I tried to get my firm to buy in but they thought it was too risky. Now I get to tell them—I told you so."

Sameer relaxed. The guy's interest in Nisha was business. "Your loss is our gain." He held up his tumbler and the guy clinked his own glass of wine to it.

"Hey, if you don't mind me asking, are you and Nisha together, you know… romantically?"

Sameer tightened his grip on the tumbler. "Why do you ask?"

"It's just we were seeing each other for a bit and

then she ghosted me. At first, I figured she was busy with the show but it's been a while and I just want to know."

"Know what?"

"Whether she's moved on or if I still have a chance. We had a good thing going. I'm in my late thirties, y'know. Tired of this dating game. There aren't many smart, beautiful women around here."

Before Sameer could respond, Aidan set down his drink. "She's finally alone. Nice meeting you."

Nisha was looking around the room, no doubt for him. He watched as Aidan hurried over to her and kissed her on the cheek. Aidan briefly placed a hand on the small of her back and Sameer remembered the feel of her silky skin under his fingers. The glass of whiskey burned a hole in his hand. Nisha smiled warmly at Aidan.

What am I doing with her? He swirled the amber liquid in the glass. It was only a matter of time before he slipped. His brother managed multiple hotels and other smaller businesses. He had a wife, young daughter and the entire family to manage. Sameer could barely handle the New York hotel and Nisha's company.

Was he being fair asking her to wait for him to come around to the idea of marriage? For as long as he'd known her, Nisha had wanted nothing more than to have a family with a loving husband and three children. He'd already taken away her ability to have children. Did he really want to string her along when there were guys like Aidan who wanted to settle down like she did? It had always been too convenient to make excuses for his bad behavior. He was being selfish thinking it was okay to be with Nisha. He didn't deserve her.

He put the tumbler of whiskey to his lips but before he could drink, his phone buzzed, startling him. The whiskey spilled onto his sleeve.

He took a breath and set the tumbler down on a table and moved away from it. It was Arjun calling. It's as if his brother had a sixth sense for when Sameer was about to screw up.

"Why did I just get a call from the Australian consulate that the hotel room of one of the members of their staff is being searched?"

Sameer cursed under his breath. "The police had a warrant," he objected, but he knew he'd made a major blunder. He should have asked whose room it was and then called their lawyer and the consulate in New York City to make sure that no one in the suite had diplomatic immunity. They did a lot of business with Australia and couldn't afford to lose it.

"I'm on my way to New York." His brother hung up without a goodbye and Sameer gave the bar one more look before making his way to Nisha to tell her he had to leave.

Nisha watched Sameer from the corner of her eye and was glad to have an excuse to end the conversation with Aidan. She met Sameer halfway and was about to tell him about the news the magazine editor had given about featuring Nisha but stopped at the look on his face.

"I need to leave. There's a situation at the hotel. I'll send the car back for you."

"I'll come with you. I was planning to stay at the hotel tonight anyway."

He looked at Aidan, who was still hovering nearby. "Don't you want to spend some more time with your friend?"

Is he serious? Sameer couldn't really think there was still something between her and Aidan. Why was he was behaving so strangely?

"Aidan is someone I dated briefly. There's nothing between us anymore."

"It didn't look that way to me."

What was going on with him? "Are you trying to pick a fight with me?" When he didn't answer, she grabbed his arm. "Let's go."

Their conversation in the car had been weighing on her all night and his current behavior didn't help.

They walked silently to the elevator. Once in the small space she caught a whiff of whiskey. "Have you been drinking?" She hadn't meant to sound accusatory but the sudden change in his demeanor was rattling her.

He stared at her. "I thought about it, but no."

Her mouth soured. "What's going on, Sameer?"

He shrugged and looked away from her.

"Why did you come close?"

"That's going to happen from time to time. And technically, I'm allowed to drink." The elevator doors opened and he walked out briskly. She had to run to catch up to him.

For the second time that night, she felt him distancing himself from her. Was this the beginning of the end between them? Had all the talk of commitment gotten too real for him? They stood in the cold air waiting for the town car to pull up to the driveway.

"Do you want me to come to the hotel with you?"

He shook his head. "I think it's best if you go home."

Sixteen

The coffee burned in his stomach but he took another sip as he looked at Arjun across the breakfast table. Sameer was used to his brother yelling at him, berating him, reminding him of just how much Sameer disappointed him. What he wasn't used to was his brother's silence.

Arjun had arrived in New York City in the middle of the night. After leaving the party, Sameer had rushed to the hotel to deal with the situation with his guests and the NYPD. As it was, none of the individuals in the room had diplomatic immunity; they were friends of the diplomats. The hotel lawyer said they would've allowed the search to continue anyway, and nothing had been found by the NYPD.

The Mahal Group was a big donor of the New York City Police Foundation, the major charity arm of the NYPD, and Sameer had called his contact there and found out that there was no need for concern. The NYPD had to follow any and all leads when it came to threats of terrorism, no matter how flimsy, and this had proved to be a false alarm.

Sameer had personally apologized to the Australians, and comped their one-month stay. The bill was tens of thousands of dollars but it was a drop in the bucket of what the country spent at their hotel.

By the time Arjun arrived, everything was handled, so his brother had chosen a bedroom and retired for the night. Sameer hadn't been able to sleep all night. The sight of Nisha with Aidan haunted him. It wasn't jealousy, it was a realization. She was ready for a commitment and she deserved it. She was the kind of girl that men married. It wasn't fair for him to keep her from achieving that dream with someone else. He'd wreaked enough havoc in her life. What had he been thinking getting into a relationship with her?

Sameer stared at the room service pancakes that were getting cold between him and Arjun. His brother had barely said two words to him.

Sameer broke the ice. "Look, I know last night was a bit of a cluster but I handled it. There's nothing left for you to do here so let's get the lecture over with."

Arjun sat up straighter and his honey-colored

eyes softened. "You've made me proud, Sameer. Yes, you messed up, but you fixed it. You handled the situation even better than I could have. You've come a long way."

His brother had never spoken to him with such sincerity. Usually, their relationship consisted of Sameer deflecting his brother's criticism with sarcasm and humor.

"But I am worried about you." Arjun took a sip of his coffee.

Here it comes.

"When I arrived, there was a slight smell of whiskey on you. Have you been drinking?"

Sameer sighed. Not Arjun too. He'd been too busy and tired to change his shirt last night.

He shook his head. "I was at a party and I came close, but I didn't."

His brother looked skeptical and Sameer didn't blame Arjun. That was exactly the kind of explanation he had given all his life for his bad behavior.

"I think you should come with me to Vegas for a few days."

So you can keep an eye on me. He knew his family meant well. If it hadn't been for them, he would never have figured out that he had a problem, and worked to fix it. But they also added tons of stress to his life. It had been hard enough when it was just a few major hotels in India. Now they had Vegas, New York City and one planned in Washington, DC. Arjun had a lot on his plate. As the eldest, he took most of the family responsibility but he also expected a lot of Sameer without once asking if it was what Sameer wanted.

"I am fine. I don't need a break and I definitely do not need an intervention."

Arjun sighed. "It's nothing like that. Divya and Ethan are coming. We want to talk to you about Nisha. Ma is on the warpath to get you married and we want to make sure you aren't feeling pressured. We just want to check in and make sure you're doing okay."

How is this not an intervention? Sameer knew how his family worked. He'd been part of one such intervention with Divya not that long ago when she wanted to marry Ethan. They all got together and tried to talk sense into the offending child. He was the one who had brought brevity and common sense into that conversation. Who would be on his side this time?

"I've got a lot to do here."

"I checked in with Vinod. He feels comfortable returning to the hotel. Nisha's company is in good shape and she's got some really competent new staff. He'll keep an eye on things." Arjun reached out and put a hand on his shoulder. "Most importantly, Simmi misses her *chacha* and would like to see him."

Sameer knew his brother was manipulating him but Arjun had him. Simmi was Arjun's little daughter. She'd had a tough beginning in life with a heart defect that needed surgery. The entire family had rallied around Arjun and Rani. Now Simmi was out of the woods and a precociously adorable toddler. Simmi was starting to talk and the way she called Sameer *chacha*—the Hindi word for father's younger brother—made him melt. Plus, he wasn't about to admit this to Arjun but he did need a break. From the hotel and from Nisha. He needed to get his head and heart together. Last night had scared him.

"If you guys gang up on me, I'm outta there. I don't care if I have to fly in the middle seat of the back row in economy."

Arjun laughed. "I don't think you've ever flown economy in your life. Might do you some good."

As much as Sameer had resisted coming to Vegas with his brother, he immediately felt at home when he entered the penthouse suite of the Mahal hotel. It was decorated similarly to the New York hotel; Rani had replicated the Vegas penthouse in New York so that traveling family members were comfortable in both places. Vegas had become Arjun and Rani's home and walking into it was a warm hug. There were adorable pictures on the wall of Simmi, and of each family member.

Sameer remembered when Arjun had wanted to break his engagement to Hema and marry Rani. His stuffy parents felt that Rani didn't have it in her to pull the family together. They couldn't have been more wrong about his sister-in-law. His *bhabhi* had made this hotel penthouse so welcoming to all of them that it felt even more like home than their grand house in India. The kitchen always had something cooking on the stove, and best of all, the pitter-patter of Simmi's feet greeted him as soon as he entered.

"Chacha!"

Sameer scooped up the little girl in his arms and kissed her on the head. She'd grown since the last time he'd seen her and he listened as she babbled on about something called *Cocomelon*. He only understood every other word in her fast-paced baby babble. Rani came over and held her arms out for her daughter but Simmi firmly shook her head. Rani laughed. "I guess you're her person today."

Sameer leaned in and kissed his sister-in-law on the cheek. "I've missed this little one. How about I watch her tonight and you guys can have a night out."

Rani put her hands together. "That would be heaven but are you sure?"

Rani ran her own interior architecture design firm, helped Arjun with their family business and raised Simmi without a full-time nanny. After what Simmi had gone through with her health issues, Rani hadn't wanted to trust her care to strangers.

"I would love it. I don't get enough time with this little *gudiya*." He kissed the top of Simmi's head. "Can I ask you a serious question, *bhabhi*? How do you do it all—the business, the family, Simmi?"

Rani smiled at him. "I don't, and neither does Arjun. We delegate. We prioritize the things that matter to us—" she looked lovingly at her daughter "—and we find competent people to handle the rest. Arjun learned that lesson the hard way—don't try to do it all yourself."

"Easier said than done."

Rani gave him a smile. "Life isn't easy." She touched his arm. "I say this with love…you are so intent on proving yourself to the family that you are micromanaging every little detail. That will burn you out. Trust your staff, and trust yourself to figure out what's important and what isn't. It doesn't matter if you make mistakes, it's about how you recover from them."

He nodded, not trusting himself to speak.

"We all love you, we're here for you, and we don't need you to prove that you're a new man. We see it every day."

He smiled gratefully at Rani once again, marveling at the fact that Arjun had ever questioned marrying this amazing woman because of his family. His *bhabhi* was smart and had a really astute way of figuring out the family dynamics.

Was she right about him? He did feel a need to prove to his family, and to Nisha if he was honest with himself, that he was a changed man. When he'd looked back at his own social media posts, he'd been embarrassed to see some of the pictures of him partying. Every time something went wrong, he thought back to those images of himself and worked twice as hard to undo that image.

Simmi wiggled out of his arms. He set her down and she led him to the living room, which was littered with toys, dolls and books. He sat on the carpet and started reading the book Simmi handed him. Having her snuggle into him almost made him want kids of his own. Almost. It was fine being uncle for the day but could he really handle being a family man?

Divya and Ethan arrived in time for dinner. Despite their rough introduction, Sameer liked Divya's fiancé. His wealth was self-made, and he treated his sister very well. Rani and Arjun had gone out to dinner and Sameer had taken charge of feeding everyone at the penthouse. He decided to use the well-appointed kitchen to make chicken biryani and raita. The beauty of living in a hotel was that he could call down to the kitchen for any ingredient Rani didn't have stocked. He'd learned to cook in rehab and after a lifetime of having his meals made for him, he enjoyed eating something made with his own hands.

He served dinner with a flourish, eliciting an eye roll from Divya. They all dug in and even the impossibly picky Simmi managed to wolf down some biryani—as long as he separated the chicken, the vegetables and rice so they were not touching each other on her plate.

After dinner he gave Simmi a bath and put her

to sleep. He returned downstairs where Divya had ordered room service coffee.

"Can you teach Ethan how to cook like that?" Divya joked as they sat down on the couch.

"Forget cooking, I want to know how you put that little terror to sleep. I work out every day and she exhausted me running around the island while you cooked," Ethan said admiringly.

"Seriously, *yaar*, you've become a regular Martha Stewart. Must be Nisha's influence." Divya winked at her brother. His heart thumped at the mention of her name. "So Ma and Reeta Auntie are planning your wedding. You know that, right?"

Sameer took a sip of his coffee. "You'd think she would've learned her lesson with you," he said lightheartedly.

Divya didn't hesitate to throw one of the decorative pillows at him. "Seriously, have you talked with Nisha about your thoughts on marriage?"

He sighed. "Yes and no. I told her I needed time."

Divya gave Sameer an exasperated look that Arjun would've been proud of.

"You know very well that now that the families are involved, your grace time has expired. You have to decide where your relationship is headed."

"So now I'm on Indian Standard Time? Two dates and a decision on the rest of my life?"

Once again Divya let out an exasperated sigh. He knew he was being purposefully obtuse but he resented the intrusion into his relationship. "It's okay to say you're not interested in marrying Nisha. It's even okay to say that it will be a long engagement."

"Aren't you the one who said I shouldn't jump into marriage? That I needed to give myself more time? How is it fair to make promises when I don't know if I can keep them?"

Divya softened her voice. "You knew from the moment you started seeing Nisha that it would come to this. What's not fair is you not committing one way or the other. After everything we've been through with that family, you can't just keep dating if you aren't eventually going to marry her."

"I want to make sure I can be the man she deserves." His voice cracked and Divya moved close to him. She placed a hand on his arm.

"That's not your call, it's hers. She will decide whether you're good enough for her. You can't take that choice away from her. Make a decision. Either give her up or make a commitment."

Divya's words hit him in the solar plexus.

"You're right. It's time I man up and do what I need to do."

Seventeen

Something wasn't right. Nisha could feel it deep in her heart. Things had been off between her and Sameer ever since the night of the fashion magazine party. He had texted her the next morning to say he was going to Vegas. Two days had gone by. He hadn't returned to New York, he hadn't called her and his text messages were getting increasingly short. Today he'd texted to say that he was returning in two days and he wanted to talk in person.

She didn't have to wait to talk to him to know what was going on. It was a pattern she was very familiar with. In college when he wanted to break up with a girl, he ignored her calls and messages, and avoided the canteen, where he might run into her.

When he'd brought up his mother's ring shopping, it was clear that he was looking for her to assure him that he didn't need to propose. He wanted her to give him a blank check. No expectations, no repercussions. She'd given him an out when the truth was that she wanted him to make a commitment. They had come a long way in their relationship. She had put a lot of trust in him after the way he'd treated her. She didn't want to end up like her mother or Aparna, in love with a man who couldn't decide what he wanted. Sameer hadn't stood up to the pressure test for their relationship. As soon as she'd become serious about commitment, he'd done what he did best: put distance between them.

She had just gotten into bed and turned off the bedside lamp when her mother knocked on the door and walked in. Nisha turned on the light and could immediately tell something was wrong. She'd just seen her mother an hour ago at dinner. Her mother had changed into her standard-issue kaftan nightgown, and her eyes were swollen and wet.

Nisha sat up. "Ma, what's wrong?"

Her mother sank down into the bed. "Your father called. He said you sent him back the money."

Plus interest.

Nisha nodded and her mother continued. "He's upset. He thinks I'm turning you against him."

Nisha closed her eyes. She'd avoided talking to her father ever since she'd talked to Aparna. Nisha knew that if she talked to him, her contempt for him would be clear.

Her mother's voice broke and Nisha sprang out of bed and got her a glass of water from the kitchen. When she returned to the bedroom, her mother was sobbing into her hands. Nisha put an arm around her.

"I'll talk to him."

She handed the glass to her mother and made her take a sip. It calmed her mother down a notch. She wiped the tears from her mother's eyes.

"I have never kept you from your father. But I cannot let you fight this battle for me. Aparna called me after you talked to her at the party."

Nisha tensed. She'd told her mother about the conversation she'd had with Aparna. "I've seen Aparna at society functions after I found out about the affair. We usually avoid each other, and when we must talk, we never talk about your father. This time Aparna was very frank. She apologized for the affair. Then she told me why things really ended with your father."

Her mother took another sip of the water and her hands trembled. "He told me it was because she wanted to end it with him for the sake of her own marriage."

Nisha wanted to throw up. Her mother needed space to tell the story her way but Nisha's sense of dread was growing every second.

"I know you don't understand why I put up with

the affair but at some level it was because I understood. Your father and Aparna fell in love before we got married. Neither he nor I had a choice in the marriage. Our parents arranged it and we were stuck with each other. I did my best to love him but I hadn't known true love. He did. She was his first love, and that's hard to forget."

Tears stung Nisha's eyes. First love. She knew all about it, knew the power it held. What if Sameer had come back into her life when she'd already married someone else? Would she have made the same decision Aparna made? "There is no excuse for him wanting to run away with her and leave you with nothing. If you got divorced in New York, you'd be entitled to half his estate yet he's made you feel thankful for every little crumb he's thrown your way. That's really why I threw the money back in his face. I need him to know that you're not beholden to him." What she really needed her father to know is that she hadn't forgiven him, and that she was now capable of taking care of herself and her mother.

"I know, I know. I put up with a lot because I wanted to keep our family together. A daughter needs her father. How would I get a good *rishta* for your marriage with shame on our house?"

Nisha rolled her eyes. "If such things are important to a man's family, I don't want to be married to him."

"*Aaare*, maybe these things don't matter in

America but in India they do. You forget that times were also different a few years ago than they are now."

They were going off topic. "Let's get back to what happened today that's upset you."

Her mother sighed. "The reason Aparna left your father is because he had another woman in his life, some socialite he met after we came here."

Nisha's mouth fell open. She didn't know whether to laugh or cry. Her cheating father had cheated on his cheating mistress?

"Then he calls me and starts yelling at me about how I haven't taught you to respect him and I couldn't take it anymore. I told him I want a divorce."

Nisha hugged her mother, a wave of relief washing over her. She had waited years for her mother to finally, finally stop putting up with her father. What she knew of their relationship was terrible. What she didn't know was probably worse. "You made the right choice. I'm glad you've finally done it." Nisha would never tell her mother just how much her parents' relationship had affected her. How lonely she'd felt her entire childhood, being the product of a loveless marriage; how the news of his affair had broken her; how watching her mother's silent tears had sown a mistrust so deep in her heart that she had trouble having faith in any man.

Then it struck her. Sameer could've left for Vegas for any number of business reasons but she had immediately jumped to the conclusion that he had an issue with their relationship.

Her mother looked at her. "I came to say sorry to you."

"To me?"

"I have been after you to get married. My parents convinced me that it was what was best for me, and I thought it was what would be best for you. I didn't want you to be alone like I had been all my life. But I am wrong. Marriage with the wrong man is worse than being alone."

Hearing her mother say those words made her heart hurt. Through every single fight with her father, her mother had been the steady one, the one to make sacrifices, the one to calm Nisha. The anger she was seeing now meant that her mother had finally broken. She hugged her mother tightly and the two women cried their eyes out.

What had Nisha been thinking wanting marriage from Sameer? Had she not learned anything from her parents' marriage? Had she forgotten her mother's years of pain and suffering? Why would she want to subject herself to something like that? There was no biological clock ticking for her and she had already spent years of emotional energy on Sameer. The only thing she needed to focus on now was her company. For her sake, and her mother's.

Eighteen

The past two days had been extra stressful. Nisha still hadn't heard from Sameer. He was officially ghosting her. Work was crazy. What she'd dreamed of just a few months ago now seemed like cruel punishment. Her studio was not big enough to accommodate the exponential growth in her staff so she had to find more space. Finding it in New York on a budget was like trying to find a grain of rice in a corn maze.

Some of the designs she had sketched weren't going to work out. The prototypes were problematic so she had to go back to the sketchbook and her creativity was on hiatus. Every time she sat down with her paper and pencil, she was totally uninspired. Her thoughts oscillated between what her mother was going through and her relationship with Sameer. It was hard to separate the two, and harder still to figure out what she wanted to do.

She had gone with her mother to a lawyer to prepare divorce documents. It would be complicated with her mother filing in New York and her father living in India. Nisha had noticed a difference in her mother once she'd signed the agreement with the lawyer to represent her. It was as if a weight had been lifted off her, and Nisha took some small pleasure in being able to pay for her mother's lawyer. For so long, her mother had made life decisions based on what Nisha needed. It felt good to give her mother the financial freedom to do what she wanted.

With a twist of her heart, she realized that she had Sameer to thank for her meteoric rise. She didn't even know half the things he'd done but she knew that a lot of designers came to New York and very few made it. Her success was not an accident and as much as she'd like to believe it was her talent, she knew it took more than that to get the kind of attention she had in a crowded fashion market. He always lifted her up, supported her, did what he could to make her successful. He was not her father.

She buried her face in her hands. What was she going to do about Sameer? She hadn't gotten over him in eight years; if he decided to leave her now, how would she ever get over him?

Lydia called out to her and she left her desk. She was tired of looking at a page full of meaningless doodles; the more she tried not to think about Sameer, the more real estate he occupied in her mind. So much so that when she heard the sound of a motorcycle, she automatically turned to the door expecting to see him.

Wait! Is that really him?

Just as he had the first time he'd come to her studio, he parked the motorcycle illegally between two cars and disembarked. Her heart lurched. When would her pulse stop jumping every time she looked at him? It had taken her years to get over him the last time. How long would it take her now?

She hadn't realized that her feet had taken her to the front door until he came breezing through it and was right in front of her.

"You can't park there. You'll get a ticket."

"I can afford it." He grinned and she wanted to lean into him, kiss him and tell him how much she'd missed him. But then she remembered her angst the past few days. She couldn't keep going like that with Sameer.

"I'm sorry I've been gone so long and didn't call you. I have a really good reason though."

I can't wait to hear what you've come up with.

She gasped as he dropped to his knees and pulled out a ring box in one sweeping move. He opened the box to reveal a diamond-encrusted wrap ring with a tastefully-sized princess-cut diamond in the center.

"Nisha, you are the first love of my life, and I'd like you to be my forever love. Will you marry me?"

She stood frozen, a lifetime of memories, a jumble of thoughts and emotions she couldn't even name coursing through her. She had been prepared to tell Sameer that marriage wasn't for her, that her father's infidelities and her mother's pain had convinced her that it wasn't worth it.

But the words he'd just spoken were probably the only ones to ground her in what she really wanted. He was her first love. He was the one she had dreamed of being with since she understood what love was. Her heart had always belonged to him. Her father hadn't had the ability to resist temptation, her mother hadn't had the courage to leave her father and Aparna couldn't give up her first love. If there was one thing she'd learned from the unhappy love triangle, it was that love mattered and happiness required risk and courage. She had taken a lot of risks with her company. It was time to do the same with her life.

"Are you going to leave him on the floor?" someone shouted and Nisha turned to see that the entire staff was behind her, standing frozen in suspense.

"I'll make him wait as long as I need. He's not the one with the bad knees," she shouted back. Her crew laughed and when she turned back, Sameer was grinning at her.

"I will stay at your feet forever. As long as the answer is yes."

She should feel bad about making him wait, but she didn't. He'd made her wait eight years. But then she locked eyes with him and he could see her answer plain as day.

"Yes, the answer is yes."

The entire studio burst into applause. Sameer stood, grabbed her face and kissed her hard. Just as the applause and hoots died, he slipped the ring onto her finger.

"What happened to the honking diamond your mother bought?"

He shrugged. "It didn't seem like something you'd like."

He was right. She hated ostentatious jewelry, and the modern ring he'd picked out with a one-carat diamond was perfect. "That's why I didn't talk to you when I was in Vegas, I was searching the entire town for just the right ring. I'm not sure I could've kept this from you."

"You know I was going crazy thinking you were going to break up with me."

He gave her a serious look and shook his head. "I can't live without you, and I don't intend to."

* * * * *

WE HOPE YOU ENJOYED
THIS BOOK FROM

⊞HARLEQUIN
DESIRE

*Luxury, scandal, desire—welcome to
the lives of the American elite.*

Be transported to the worlds of oil barons, family dynasties,
moguls and celebrities. Get ready for juicy plot twists,
delicious sensuality and intriguing scandal.

6 NEW BOOKS AVAILABLE EVERY MONTH!

#2905 THE OUTLAW'S CLAIM

Westmoreland Legacy: The Outlaws • by Brenda Jackson

Rancher Maverick Outlaw and Sapphire Bordella are friends with occasional benefits. But when Phire must marry at her father's urging, their relationship ends...until they learn she's carrying Maverick's baby. Now he'll stop at nothing to stake his claim...

#2906 CINDERELLA MASQUERADE

Texas Cattleman's Club: Ranchers and Rivals • by LaQuette

Ready to break out of her shell, Dr. Zanai James agrees to go all out for the town's masquerade ball and meets handsome rancher Jayden Lattimore. Their attraction is instantaneous, but can their connection survive meddling families bent on keeping them apart?

#2907 MARRIED BY MIDNIGHT

Dynasties: Tech Tycoons • by Shannon McKenna

Ronnie Moss is in trouble. The brilliant television host needs a last-minute husband to fulfill her family's marriage mandate before she turns thirty— at midnight. Then comes sexy stranger Wes Brody, who volunteers himself. But is this convenient arrangement too good to be true?

#2908 SNOWED IN SECRETS

Angel's Share • by Jules Bennett

After distillery owner Sara Hawthorne and Ian Ford spend one hot night together, they don't expect to see each other again...until he shows up for their scheduled interview about her family business. Now snowed in, can they keep it professional?

#2909 WHAT HAPPENS AFTER HOURS

404 Sound • by Kianna Alexander

Recording studio exec Miles Woodson needs a showstopping act for his charity talent show, and R & B superstar Cambria Harding fits the bill. But when long days working together become steamy nights, can these opposites make both their passion project and relationship work?

#2910 BAD BOY WITH BENEFITS

The Kane Heirs • by Cynthia St. Aubin

Sent to audit his distillery, Marlowe Kane should keep her distance from bad boy owner Law Renaud. But when a storm prevents her from getting home, they can't resist, and their relationship awakens a passion in both that could cost them everything...

HDCNM0922

*Returning to her hometown, brokenhearted journalist
Adaline Harlow is supposed to write an exposé on
Colter Ward, Texas's Sexiest Bachelor, and that
assignment does not include falling for him! As the
attraction grows, will they break their no-love-allowed
rule for a second chance at happiness?*

Read on for a sneak peek at
Most Eligible Cowboy
by USA TODAY bestselling author Stacey Kennedy.

"You want your story. I want these women off my back…
Stay in town and agree to being my girlfriend until this
story dies down and I'll give you the exclusive you want."

"Her eyes widened. "You're serious?"

"Deadly serious," he confirmed. "I want my life back.
You need a promotion. This is a win-win for both of us."

She gave a cute wiggle on her stool. "I think you're
giving me far too much credit. Why would women care if
I'm your girlfriend?"

"I don't think you're giving yourself enough credit."
He stared at her parted lips, shining eyes, her slowly

building smile, and closed the distance between them, waiting for her to back away. When she didn't and even leaned in closer, he said, "Trust me, they'd care." He captured her mouth, cupping her warm face, telling himself the whole damn time this was a terrible idea.

Don't miss what happens next in...
Most Eligible Cowboy
by USA TODAY *bestselling author Stacey Kennedy.*

Available November 2022 wherever
Harlequin Desire books and ebooks are sold.

Harlequin.com